THE HIDING-
PLACE

Other books by Lyn Cook:

The Bells on Finland Street
The Little Magic Fiddler
Rebel on the Trail
Jady and the General
Pegeen and the Pilgrim
The Road to Kip's Cove
Samantha's Secret Room
The Brownie Handbook of Canada
The Secret of Willow Castle
The Magical Miss Mittens
A Treasure for Tony

Picture-books:

Toys from the Sky
Jolly Jean Pierre
If I Were All These
The Magic Pony
Sea Dreams

LYN COOK
THE HIDING-PLACE

Lester Publishing Limited

Canadian Cataloguing in Publication Data

Cook, Lyn
   The hiding-place

ISBN 1-895555-76-0

I. Title.

| PS8505.O66H54 | 1994 | jC813'.54 | C94-930990-7 |
| PZ7.C66Hi | 1994 | | |

Lester Publishing Limited
56 The Esplanade
Toronto, Ontario
Canada M5E 1A7

Printed and bound in Canada

94 95 96 97 5 4 3 2 1

Dedicated with devotion
to the memory of my husband,
Robb John Waddell,
whose loving support
made all my books possible;

to the family we shared,
Deborah, Christopher, and Anne;
and especially to our grandson,
Matthew Robb

Acknowledgements

The author wishes to express her gratitude to all those who were of assistance to her and this book on its way to publication: to Linda Sheppard for early approval and input; to Carol Ives and the staff of the Bendale Branch of the Scarborough Public Library, in particular Sylvia Simpson, for invaluable support with research and encouragement; to Gillian Misener, her niece, for translation; to Kenneth Lister of the Royal Ontario Museum for facts relating to the Montagnais; to John Thompson, wildlife biologist; to Ian McGregor of the McLaughlin Planetarium; and to those special advisers who helped her chart a course through the shoals of syntax and content, her editors, Kathy Lowinger and Kirsten Hanson.

Contents

1   Escape to Freedom   1

2   Footsteps in the Dark   8

3   A Strange Hideaway   18

4   A Cave on the River   29

5   The Boy Is Dying!   42

6   A Fall Down the Cliff   55

7   Captured!   66

8   A Rainbow in the Night   83

9   Tunnel to Safety   93

10   The Whales Have Come!   103

11   "There's somebody up there!"   113

12   A Voyager Returns   126

13   Farewell to Friend and Forest   135

CHAPTER ONE

Escape to Freedom

She was safely hidden; that was all that mattered. Who would ever think to search for her in Monsieur Rivard's abandoned well? The old man had been gone for a long time. He had left the settlement to return home to France when his young wife and son had died of the fever. She tried to control her shivering. How cold and dank the well was, and dark! And what if the fever lurked in its empty depths? But wasn't she high enough above the well bottom, crouched on the shelf that Monsieur Rivard had made for summer storage? Anyway, it was better to take a chance on illness, even of the dreaded fever, than to suffer unnameable horrors in the home of Louis Gaudin. She would never go back there, no matter what Gervaise said. When would he come? *Please, God, let it be soon. Please, Holy Mary, Mother of God!*

Had Denis been able to deliver the note to Gervaise? It should have been easy enough. It was only on her that Monsieur Gaudin kept an ever-watchful eye, as if he had a suspicion of her intention to escape. Those eyes! How she loathed those eyes! Narrow and scheming when he and she were alone together in the cabin, but wide with innocence and good will when someone from the village was about.

Then she heard the whistle, long and low like that of a lone night-bird. Quickly she whistled a reply and in a moment Gervaise's hand was reaching down to grasp hers as she climbed up the jagged stones of the well wall.

"Justine! What are you doing here?"

"Shh! Not so loud. Did anyone see you come?" She glanced fearfully down the bush trail.

"Not a soul. And I told no one of your note. But what are you doing here?" he repeated. "I heard Monsieur Gaudin asking about the village if anyone had seen you."

"Gervaise, I won't go back there again! You mustn't tell anyone I'm here!"

"Of course, if that's what you wish. But why?"

"He means me harm. Please, don't make me speak of it."

"Harm? Louis Gaudin?" Even in the dark she could see the astonished look on Gervaise's face as he drew close to her. "You can't mean that. He has given you and your brother a home."

"You see? You don't believe me." She began to cry quietly, despairingly, muffling her sobs in her cloak. "No one would believe me!"

Gervaise placed an arm gently about her shoulders and drew her close. "Justine, don't cry. Tell me."

"It's the way he looks at me. The way he reaches out to me. How can I speak of it?"

"You don't need to. Not to me."

"Yes, but who else would believe me? Monsieur Gaudin gave money to bring the new young priest out from the old country. He gave the new baptismal font to the church. Who would believe me?" She clung to him without hope.

Gervaise was silent for a moment. "I believe you. Has he harmed you?"

Justine was surprised at the harshness in his voice. It had the authority of a man much older than sixteen. "Gervaise, last night he'd been drinking *bouillon*, Monsieur Marchand's homemade beer. He was worse than ever when he came home. I thought he might...." She paused, trembling.

"Did he do anything to you? Tell me!"

"No, but I was afraid he would. I had to get away, and at once. I can't take a chance any more. If I stayed there I would always be afraid of him. And then, Madame Sagard and Madame Couteau have it in mind that I shall marry him. They think that would be the best for all of us!"

"You? Marry Louis Gaudin?" Gervaise drew back and stared at her. "What kind of nonsense is this?"

"It isn't nonsense. I heard them talking when I took back the pot Madame Couteau had brought us soup in. I heard Madame Sagard say that I was, after all, nearly thirteen, and that the Sieur de Champlain himself had married a twelve-year-old." She knew who the Sieur de Champlain was. He had sailed many years ago from the port of Honfleur, where her family had set sail four years before. He had come in search of a route to the fabled Indies, and had instead found the great river St. Lawrence, and the fur fort of Tadoussac, where they lived. Well, let him marry a twelve-year-old. That was nothing to do with her. "They said that I could be a servant in his home for one or two years, then all could be arranged."

"Arranged! Could it indeed?" Gervaise exploded angrily. "They're a pair of busybodies who should mind their own business. There's a ship arriving from France in August, with orphans and widows aboard. I understand one of them is to be his wife."

"Not the way they see it. Madame Sagard said Monsieur Gaudin has even spoken to her about me. And they were both nodding their heads and agreeing that since he has taken Denis and me in it would be a fine arrangement for us all." She buried her face in his shoulder. "Gervaise, I am never, never going back! He's so terrible!"

Gervaise took her hands firmly in his. "I'll help you all I can. But if you're planning to hide on the edge of the wilderness, what about the Iroquois?"

The Iroquois! How they all feared the Iroquois! But it had been a different kind of enemy that had come in the night and destroyed their home and family, a spark from the chimney that set the roof thatch ablaze. "I won't be afraid of the Indians. I'll keep hidden. The Blessed Virgin will protect me."

"But there's Denis. He'll be lonely without you."

"He'll be all right, I know he will. He helps Monsieur Gaudin about the land and the barn, and if there's a marriage when the ship comes with the widows and orphans from France, surely the new wife will look after my brother."

"Yes, and I can keep an eye out for him and make sure he's well treated." Gervaise considered. "Now, tell me what you plan."

"I know what I want to do. I want to live on the edge of the village, quite hidden, until the ship comes from France. Then, somehow, I'll smuggle myself aboard and go upriver to Quebec. The nuns at the Ursuline convent there will take me in. If the choice is to marry Monsieur Gaudin, I'd rather be a nun." She remembered that when her cousin Madeleine, at home in France, had refused to marry the man her parents had chosen for her, she had been sent to a convent. "I'll gladly go to a convent, Gervaise, oh, so gladly!"

"You may have a long wait here, Justine. It's only July. How will you live?"

"With your help. You will help me, won't you, Gervaise? We came to New France from the same town in the old country. We've grown up together here in Tadoussac. You've been like a brother to me!"

"Of course I'll help you. Have you eaten today?"

"Yes. I stuffed some bread and cheese in my reticule. But I'll need more. And Gervaise, can you bring some of your younger brother's clothes, ones he's outgrown?"

"If I can find some that Maman has not made quilts of. You'll be a boy, then?"

"Yes. Justin, not Justine. It's safer that way. And could you bring some shears to cut my hair? Down to the waist is too long for a boy!"

"A little, yes." Gervaise stroked the fine blonde tresses gently. "Still, it does seem a great shame to take away your hair. It's beautiful!"

She looked up at him in surprise. "But it will grow again. And besides, if I'm a nun it must all be cut off."

Gervaise spoke rather solemnly. "There's a long time yet for you to become a nun. We'll wait and see what happens." He rose and helped her to her feet. "And now I must be going or they'll wonder where I've got to." He approached the edge of the well. "Come, I want to see you safely down before I go. It's dangerous out here in the dark."

She clung to his hand before she began to climb down. "Oh, Gervaise, if only it hadn't happened. If only things could be as they were three weeks ago."

"Have courage, little friend. Say your prayers and wait for me. I'll be back tomorrow night when it's dark."

And then he was gone, swallowed up by the trees and the intense darkness of the forest. In the well she was suddenly aware of the awful silence around her, and then, as she listened, she heard the night sounds come to life, the hoot of an owl, the lone far-off cry of a wolf on the ridge, the scutterings of small animals looking for shelter or food. The noises gave her a strange comfort. She was not alone in the night. She wrapped her cloak more closely about her and curled up in a ball, trying to picture the home she had lost, so that she would never forget it in the years to come. It hadn't mattered that there had been only one room for all of them. It contained all they needed, the wooden bunks for Denis and herself, Maman's spinning wheel and loom for making warm woollen clothing, the long pine table and benches, and the canopied bed Papa and Maman had brought from France, piled high with woollen blankets. Beside that were the cradles of the two babies close to Maman's hand. Then there was the cheery open fire with the flagstone hearth and the hooks for the pots and pans, the stockpots and stewbasins, and the great black iron cauldron on a spit over the flames, always filled with delicious soup. And on a ledge over the hearth were the set of flatirons, the tin lamps, and the candlesticks. The hearth was the centre of the home and of their lives, she thought. But then she remembered with horror that the fire that destroyed everything had come from that very hearth.

How could she ever look on fire as a source of comfort again, when it had taken all she loved? Maman, Papa, and the beloved babies, Céleste and Nicolas—all except Denis, dead. Even the barns and animals had gone, the piglets and the two sows, the milk cow and the two sheep. Only the oxen, close to the barn door, had managed to break through to safety, bellowing their fear.

She clutched her grandmother's necklace of ruby red beads. It was the only thing they had found intact among the bent and twisted pewter mugs and porringers, the turnspit crane and pothooks from the hearth. Someone had told her that the oiled paper covering the windows had only added to the fury of the blaze. If they had had proper windows and their home had been built of whitewashed stone as Papa had planned for the future, they might have been saved. But a log house went up in flames like a woodpile if a spark escaped from the hearth and ignited the pine floor, or flew up the chimney to settle on the thatched roof.

She tried to still her trembling and began to count the red beads like a rosary, coming at last to the silver clasp. She knew what was there—the date of her mother's birth in faraway France, June 4, 1610, and her grandmother's and grandfather's initials intertwined. She would never never lose the necklace. It would be her charm for survival, her memory of a life that could never be again. Clutching it close, she fell asleep.

When she wakened with a start she was stiff with cold. Where was she? The well! She was hiding in Monsieur Rivard's well! How dark and horrible it was. But what had wakened her? It had been a noise, but what? Was it the Iroquois on a swift raid in the night? Monsieur Gaudin come in search of her? She heard a loud snuffle, and saw the enormous form making shadows on the well wall. A bear! It was only a bear from the forest that had found her scent. But there was no way it could get down the well, no matter how it snuffled and snorted. She was safe here from wild animals. She watched, fascinated, while the huge body wove back and forth around the well opening. Then suddenly the bear was gone, lumbering off into the trees. She gave a deep sigh, breathing thanks to God for her safety, and settled herself again in the folds of her cloak, running her fingers over and over the ruby red beads. The midnight sky was her bed canopy, studded with sparkling stars. If she tried to count them, sleep would come more quickly, and daylight, and Gervaise.

CHAPTER TWO

Footsteps in the Dark

When she wakened next, the first faint glimmer of light and warmth was beginning to penetrate the deep chill of the well. Her limbs were cramped from the cold and the twisted position she had been forced to lie in on the shelf. She stretched cautiously, afraid of falling into the slimy water far below. Then she devoured the last of her bread and cheese, longing for hot milk or soup to go with them. Gervaise would not come till dark; the day before her seemed endless. She tried to imagine the life of the village, the early-morning prayers as each family rose to start a new day, the trips to the well for fresh water, the quick breakfasts of wholemeal porridge and bread and milk before the men and children set to work side by side on the land, and the women at the spinning wheel and loom, or at the hearth, cooking and baking. She could almost smell the fragrant bread as her mother carried it, round and steaming, from the outdoor oven to the cabin. She could eat a whole loaf of it herself right now! Better not to think about that. She must decide where she was going to hide until the next ship came in, and how she could smuggle herself aboard for the long journey up the river to Quebec and the safety of the convent.

There was no haven across the St. Lawrence River. The other shore was far away, and it was also the known haunt of the Iroquois, who had come over more than once to attack the settlements on the north shore. If only there were a hiding-place in the fort buildings! But she could remember none, even though she had been there a few times with Papa, the head clerk. The fort itself had been a refuge for all the villagers and those Montagnais Indians who lived on the outskirts of the settlement, when they feared an Iroquois attack, but it was hardly enough protection. The wooden stockade and log buildings inside were too exposed to firebrands and flaming arrows. The storehouse of muskets and gunpowder for the defence of the fort made it even more dangerous. That certainly wasn't a good place to hide. Then, with a rush of excitement, she remembered Monsieur Picard, who had taken his family to the town of Quebec in search of a safer life. He had abandoned his cabin under the sand ridge. Perhaps she could shelter there. She could hardly wait to ask Gervaise what he thought about that.

As the day wore on she listened to the birds in the forest beside her secret place and tried to distinguish their calls. She heard the pure liquid notes of thrushes, the raucous shrieks of jays, and the persistent hammering of a woodpecker. And then she heard another sound— footsteps! She froze with fear, but they passed quickly, their owner whistling like the birds. A hunter from the village, no doubt, on his way to find deer meat for his family. She hoped there was no Indian in wait for him, or he would not be seen again.

Dark came at last, with the far-off sound of the angelus bell from the village church and the distant shimmer of stars spangling the heavens. She noticed one great star shining, perhaps, just for her. She thought it might be a sign of God's help, to light her difficult way.

"Justine, I'm here!"

Gervaise at last. She reached up her hand and he drew her beside him on the long grass. "I found it hard to get away. Monsieur Gaudin stopped me in front of the captain of the militia's house, wanting to talk about your disappearance. He's really angry that you'd do such a foolish thing."

"Gervaise, you didn't...."

"Of course I didn't, little goose." He ruffled her hair playfully. "What do you take me for? I haven't said a word to anyone, although there's plenty of talk around the village."

"What are they saying?"

"Oh, things like what a pity you'd repay Monsieur Gaudin's kindness by running away; that because they've failed to find you with everyone searching, the wolves must have devoured you, or the Indians taken you away."

"There! What did I tell you? They're all on his side."

"Not all. Look who's come to you tonight." He grinned at her in the dark. "And with lots of food for you to eat, and clothes for your disguise. How do you like that?"

"Oh, Gervaise, I do love you for this." She reached out and gave him a swift hug.

"I'll remind you of that one day." Gervaise assumed a mock-serious manner. "And now, boy, how short will you have your hair?" He held up a pair of shears.

"Perhaps here." She pointed to an area just below the nape of her neck. "And I can tie it with a leather thong like yours."

It was done in a moment. She felt horror-stricken as she saw the shining strands in Gervaise's hands. He saw the look on her face. "Fine stuffing for a cushion," he joked. But she noticed that he placed the tresses carefully in his deerskin bag as if he treasured them. Then he brought out the food.

"You'll be starving. I've brought plenty to last you through tomorrow, and a flagon of fresh water."

He spread an astonishing feast before her on the grass: a small, round *tourtière* that he said was of pork and rabbit, another pie made of wild partridge and herbs, cooked turnip and cabbage, cold salt bacon, and the large plump loaf of bread she had longed for.

"Gervaise, how did you manage all this?"

"Oh, I have my ways. And I got along with a little less in the fields today. Is it enough?"

"More than enough." She ate hungrily. "I'll save some in case you find it hard to come tomorrow. You will come, won't you?"

"Nothing shall stop me, I promise. But what about a better hiding-place?"

In her eagerness to share her plan she found she was trying to eat and speak at the same time. "You remember Monsieur Picard, who took his family upriver to safety? What about his cabin under the ridge? I know it's tumbling down and raccoons and woodchucks and foxes have found their way in, but I can live with them."

"I have a better idea. What do you say to the haystack *behind* the cabin? Someone might take shelter in the cabin in a storm, but no one would go to the haystack with the cabin nearby."

"Oh, I like that, Gervaise!"

"You can hollow out a place for yourself and line it with tree branches. It will be warm and dry."

"I'll do it. Just before dawn tomorrow, before the village is really awake, I'll move. I'll creep along the edge of the forest."

"You should be safe there. I hear the Iroquois have been fighting the Montagnais up in the hills, but no one has seen them by the river. They've probably gone up the Saguenay with their booty and prisoners. Now, what about these clothes? I hope they fit. You and my brother Marc seem to be the same size. You're not very big, you know."

No, she was not very big. Small of frame and oval of face like her grandmother, they said, but with the fair hair and brown eyes of beloved Maman. She reached for the clothes—coarse breeches made of hemp, a rough linen shirt with a brown deerskin jerkin, and long woollen stockings. Her own cloak would go well over these.

Gervaise produced a knitted cap from his bag. "You can tuck this away in case of cold, and wear your own wooden clogs."

"What about my voice, Gervaise?"

"Just like Marc's. I couldn't tell the difference if I didn't know you. You'll make a fine boy, Justine."

"Justin! If I meet a stranger, I'm Justin."

"Good for you! Justin it shall be." He laid his hands warmly on hers. "I promise I'll look after you as long as I can, and may that be until we find a new home and a new life for you!"

"Gervaise, before you go, please tell me no one has seen you come, no one has followed you here. You're *sure*?"

"Quite sure. I'm making the evening rounds checking the animals in the field and barn last a little longer, that's all. No one knows I've come."

It was only a moment after he had slipped away silently into the night that she had reason to doubt his word. She had finished hastily changing her clothes and was burrowing down in her cloak for warmth when she heard a noise. Footsteps! Coming towards the well!

Monsieur Gaudin—it must be! He had followed Gervaise and found her. She waited, scarcely breathing. The whisper, when it came, was frantic.

"Justine, are you there?"

Denis! It was her brother Denis, not Monsieur Gaudin. What was *he* doing here?

"Denis, how did you find me? Why did you come?"

"Justine, let me come down. *Please* let me!"

"You must go back. This is no place for you!"

"I won't go back. I've watched Gervaise for two days. I knew he was bringing you things. Justine, I want to be with you!"

"But Monsieur Gaudin will look after you. He means you no harm."

"I won't stay with him. He's angry that you ran away and says he'll make me tell him where you are! I'm afraid of him, Justine."

How could she refuse Denis?

"Come down, then, but tread carefully on the well stones. There's not much room on the shelf here." She stood and guided him down beside her and then drew him into her arms. "Oh, Denis, you should have stayed where it was safe."

He began to sob, his face hidden against her cloak. "I want to be with you. Why did the fire come, Justine? And where have Maman and Papa gone, and little Céleste and baby Nicolas?"

"You know they've gone to heaven to be with God, Mousekin. Don't cry now. I'll look after you." But how could she, with the dangers of the wilderness all around them? Well, he would have to learn to obey.

"If you're staying with me you must do exactly as I say, like a soldier. Do you promise?"

"I promise. Anything, as long as you don't send me back."

"Then now is the time for sleep. Crawl under my cloak and I'll keep you warm."

As he did so, he peered at her in astonishment through the darkness. "Justine, you're dressed like a boy!"

"Yes, and a boy I shall be. From now on my name is Justin. Will you remember?"

"Justin. I'll try." Denis thought a minute; then his face brightened. "Just like Justin Bouchard, who helped Papa sort and clean the furs at the fort."

"Just like him. Now you must sleep. Would you like me to sing about King Dagobert?"

"Oh, I'd like that, Justine."

"Justin!"

"Justin. I'll remember. I promise!"

She began the old nursery song, and as she crooned the words she could hear her grandmother's voice in faraway France lovingly amusing her at bedtime so long ago.

> King Dagobert once wore
> His breeches turned hindside before.
> Said Eloi, the friar:
> "Oh, my King and Sire,
> Those fine clothes on you
> Are all wrong side to!"
> The King said, "You don't say?
> Then I'll turn them the other way!"

She felt a tremor as Denis gave a little giggle, and then she thought he was asleep. But suddenly he stirred and said quietly, "Justin, are Maman and Papa watching over us from heaven?"

"They are, Mousekin. I know they are." They needed to be, she thought, and all the saints above, if she and Denis were to survive. "Sleep now."

And they did sleep, until Denis wakened with a start as the stars were fading, and complained of the cold. She bundled him more tightly in the cloak. "It will be morning soon, and the sun will shine down on us."

"Justine. Justin," he corrected himself hastily. "Why doesn't Michel come back? He could look after us."

Yes, Michel could look after them. Their older brother would be the answer now, if he hadn't run away more than two years before to join the runners of the woods, the *coureurs de bois* who ventured into the wilderness to set up their own private fur trade with the Indians.

"Why did he go? Why did he run away?"

"Because he wanted adventure, Denis. He was there when the *coureurs de bois* came to Papa to have him make their wills before they started on their journey. He heard their stories and longed to go."

"Why did they do that? Make their wills, I mean."

"Because they knew some of them might never come back. They have to travel many leagues, Denis, through enemy Indian country where wild animals live and where huge rivers run with rapids and waterfalls."

She felt him stiffen. "Then Michel will never come back?"

"Of course he'll come back." But would he? Would they ever see him again? She had almost given up hope.

"But somebody *did* see him once," Denis reminded her. "Lucien Perron told Papa when he came back from his trading trip that he'd met Pierre Tremblay many leagues away, and that Pierre said he'd met Michel. Don't you remember, Justine? Justin, I mean."

"He said that, yes, I remember." But the traveller Pierre had met had been a lone *coureur* and Michel was on the trail with several young men from the village. Michel would know the dangers of going alone in the wilderness. It was a false hope.

Denis was content. "Then he must be safe somewhere."

"Yes, he must be safe somewhere." But in her heart
she wondered. Had the wilderness devoured him, just as
fire had devoured their home and family?

"Just…." Denis paused. "Justin, why didn't Michel
say goodbye?"

"He crept away in the night because he knew Maman
and Papa wouldn't let him go if they knew."

"Why didn't they want him to go?"

"Why? Why? You're like a catechism with your
'whys'! Papa wanted him to help on the farm and in the
fort. He hoped Michel would one day be in charge there,
as he was. That's why he taught him to read and write."

Denis rubbed his eyes sleepily. "I'd like to be a
coureur de bois. They dress like Indians, in animal-skin
clothes and fur hats with tails. I'd like that."

"Yes, but sometimes they're bad company. That's
what Maman and Papa were afraid of. Remember when
four of them came back to the village last fall with all
those furs? They ate and gambled and drank all their
profits away!"

"Will Michel do that, Justin?"

"Not Michel. He'll look after us, Denis, when he
comes back." And come back he must, somehow, even
if it was more than two years since he had gone. She
must keep her hopes and faith alive, because with Denis
to look after her dreams of escaping upriver to the
convent had to be abandoned for now. "Sleep now,
Denis. It'll soon be dawn and we're going to find another
hiding-place, in Monsieur Picard's haystack."

She was drifting off herself, her arms tight around
her brother, when he spoke again, his voice heavy with
sleep. "Justine."

"Justin. Remember?"

"Justin, isn't it good that Michel ran away? If he'd stayed he would have been in the cabin too, sleeping up in the loft where the thatch caught fire."

"You're right, Denis. He's lucky to be away in the wilderness."

She hadn't thought of it that way before. Michel's flight had saved him, even if he took no trade goods to exchange for the Indians' beaver skins, no blankets or knives, no kettles or buttons or beads. But how had he, Michel, the gentle one, found the courage to go at all? Who could imagine him a fearless *coureur* in the wild forests when the greatest danger he had had to face in the settlement, barring an Iroquois attack, was the anguish of a sick or hurt animal? It had been Michel who had had the healing hands and the healing potions there. That had begun on the journey from France when, as a boy of fourteen, he had befriended the oldest woman aboard the sailing ship, Old Granny Beauchamp. Known as a healer in their town in France, she had taught a willing Michel her secrets, so that whenever an animal or person fell ill in the new village, Michel accompanied her on her errand of mercy. At sixteen he had been revered and praised for his gentleness and knowledge. And then he had gone in the night, as secretly and swiftly as the Indians he would meet on his way. He was alive somewhere; he had to be. He had joined others on a journey up the great Saguenay into the unknown. But truly, would he ever come back? Murmuring prayers for her brother's safety, she fell asleep.

CHAPTER THREE

A Strange Hideaway

"Denis! Denis, wake up!"

"Where are we?" He began to stretch beside her and she had to catch him quickly to save him from falling over the edge of the shelf.

"In the well, remember? But it's later than I wanted it to be. They'll be about in the village soon and we must be on our way."

"Where are we going, Justine?"

What was the use? "Justine" it would have to be. She would have to take her chances on that and forget the boy's name. She suddenly realized what a burden had been added to her plans for escape. "To Monsieur Picard's haystack. We talked about it last night. I'll wrap the rest of the food and my other clothes in my cloak and go up first to look about. But we must pray for God's blessing." She held tight to the ruby red necklace, again fingering it like a rosary, and, after prayers, hung it inside her linen shirt. Then she began to climb.

Their best protection was the semi-darkness that still shrouded the forest. She beckoned to Denis and helped him to a place beside her, crouched in the long grass.

"We'll bend low like this, and keep inside the fringe of trees. That way we're hidden and safe from the Indians, too. Move quickly, Denis!"

It was just light enough to see the way. Bent almost double, they ran swiftly among the trees, covering the huge half-circle of forest that bordered the village on one side. On the other, the morning light glistened on the cove waters that bordered the settlement. They could hear the distant sounds of the village awakening, the rattle of cauldron and harness, the strident crow of a rooster. Suddenly, in horror, Justine stopped short and pulled Denis into an alder thicket. "There's someone coming! I can see his shadow! Not a word!"

Monsieur Gaudin! It was Monsieur Gaudin! Justine silently prayed that he would not see them. Her plea was answered. The thin figure, face scowling in the half-light, passed the thicket. Suddenly he veered to the right, towards the abandoned cabin and the well.

"Where's he going?" Denis whispered. He shook in the cradle of her arms.

"To the well. Someone has seen where Gervaise was coming and told him."

"What will he do to us if he finds us, Justine?"

"Shh, he won't find us. We'll wait here until he's right out of sight, and then hurry on."

The light was growing stronger when they saw him pass again on his return to the village and take a shortcut away from the forest across a neighbour's corn field. "We'll be safe now. But run! Quickly and silently!" Justine warned.

Monsieur Picard had chosen a holding remote from the village. When they finally reached his haystack safely they were exhausted. They crawled inside to shelter and catch their breath. "There's no time to waste," Justine warned. "We'll make our hideaway on the side of the haystack facing the forest. Then no one will be able to see our comings and goings. There's no trail into the forest close by, so we should be safe from hunters."

When they had rested they ate some of the food from the cloak. Denis would have taken more but quickly she folded what was left into the clothes. "We have to be a little hungry, Denis, until we know what we're going to do. Gervaise may find it hard to bring food. We know now that Monsieur Gaudin has heard we're in the area. Someone may be spying on Gervaise."

"Shall we make a little house inside here, Justine?"

"Yes, a kind of little house. We'll make the hole inside the haystack larger to give us space to move about a little, and line it with pine branches. Then we can bring more branches to sleep on. It'll be much cosier than the well. You'll see."

They worked steadily through the long morning, Justine keeping an ever-watchful eye towards the village. But no one came, and by noon their hay house was complete. "It's like the pretend fort Michel made for me near the barn, Justine," Denis said. "I like it here." And before he had time to recall that that too had been devoured by fire she brought out the remains of the *tourtière* and they ate lunch.

The long day passed slowly with a quick venture outside the stack now and then to stretch their legs. Justine tried to amuse Denis with the songs and stories she remembered her grandmother sharing in faraway France long ago, but still the questions came.

"Justine, why did you run away? Why can't we go back to the village?"

"I didn't like staying with Monsieur Gaudin, Denis. They should never have let him take us in. I once heard Papa telling Maman, after we were in bed, that he felt he couldn't trust him even though he had been in the village over a year. But no one else felt the same way. He's much admired for his gifts to the church. I didn't feel safe with him, that's all. You must be content with that."

"Shall we always live like this, then?"

"Oh, no! The Blessed Virgin will help us. She'll show us the way to a new life!" But when, and how?

"Then why didn't she help Maman and Papa and the babies?"

"I told you, they're safe in heaven. She'll comfort them there." But just the same, the doubts lingered. She remembered her father's words on the voyage from France. The ocean gales rocked the ship and the sails bent to touch the waves. The passengers were in despair with illness and fear and, hatchways closed against the storm, with the stench of a hundred bodies. And yet Papa, trying to bring comfort to the stricken passengers, had led them all in prayer and told her, "God always has a measure of mercy for believers."

But where was the measure of mercy when the fire came? Where was the measure of mercy for them now? Was it the fact that she and Denis, and perhaps Michel in the wilderness, had lived? A strange mercy. Then quickly she asked forgiveness for her doubts. They were safe in a hiding-place now, and for that measure of mercy she was grateful.

The dark came again, and with it Gervaise. Again came the long, low whistle and her own reply. He crept into the haystack with them.

"Denis, you're here!" Quickly they explained why, and he understood. "It's a snug hideaway for both of you."

"Gervaise, are you sure no one saw you come?" Justine told him briefly that in the morning they had seen Monsieur Gaudin.

"I'm sure I wasn't followed. I heard Monsieur Gaudin say he'd search the entire village for you, and if he didn't find you, you deserved to be eaten by a bear or taken by the Indians." Gervaise gave her a wry half-smile. "He didn't know I heard. He was speaking to Martin—you know, the mute boy who helps him in the fields."

Justine caught sight of the food he had brought. "Gervaise, where did you get all that? Your Maman will want to know where it goes!"

"Young Jacques Sagard was to help me with the hay today, and when he didn't show up I saved the dinner Maman had sent for him." Gervaise frowned suddenly. "But it's going to get harder, Justine. You won't come back and see the priest?"

"Never! He'd say I was a disobedient child. He wouldn't understand!"

Gervaise shrugged. "Well, I'll do my best until we can think of a plan for you. Meanwhile I have news. A fur trader came into the village and told us a great ship is on its way from France. We expect it to put into our Tadoussac cove tomorrow afternoon." He looked at her questioningly.

She gave a quick, sad glance at Denis. "I can't try to get aboard now, Gervaise. Things have changed. There has to be another way. Perhaps we'll find another settlement and someone there can take us upriver to the convent by barge or canoe."

He patted her shoulder. "Perhaps. There'll be a way, I know."

"I know, too. I'll keep praying."

"Tomorrow I'm helping Robert Lavigne build his barn. All the young men will be there. So don't worry if I'm a little later coming. You have enough food now to last a while."

"We'll look for you, Gervaise. The day seems not so long when we know we'll see you at the end of it."

She watched him go, a tall, lithe figure loping through the darkness, wishing she could go with him. Denis had eyes only for the food.

"Justine, there are sweet cakes here! May I have some now?"

"Not now, Denis. We must be careful with the food. Gervaise may have trouble getting more for us." But in the end she relented and allowed him one small cake before sleep. Then she announced that it was time for evening prayers.

"Do we have to pray out here, Justine? Nobody knows."

"God knows." She tried to speak firmly without harshness. "Denis, while we hide I'm the governor here. You wouldn't disobey the governor of New France, would you?"

"Oh, no, Justine! He's like the king!"

"Then you will listen and do as I say. Pray with me now and give thanks. Always give thanks."

"I could say thank you for the little cake and maybe then I could have another."

Justine laughed aloud. "You're a scamp, Denis. Another cake tomorrow, perhaps."

When he was asleep she crept out to look at the stars. The sky was alive with them, so that the night had a summer brightness that shone even on the lapping water of the cove where the village lay, and on the vast waters of the Saguenay River that flowed out to the St. Lawrence just beyond the settlement. And behind their haystack home the huge ridge, studded with spruce, black pine, and balsam, rose high like an immense dark curtain, merging with the gigantic hills that bordered the Saguenay as far as the eye could see and rolled away into the mysterious wilderness. Perhaps Michel was out there somewhere in the wilderness, coming home. A sharp wild cry pierced the silence of the night. What was it? An Indian raid? A lone trader in trouble on his way home? Perhaps it was the pain of an animal under attack by another. She shivered and sought the shelter of the haystack, drawing her cloak around her.

As she lay down to sleep she heard mice rustling in the hay and thought of Papa at home, greasing the bunk posts with goose fat so the mice in the cabin couldn't climb into the hay mattress on her bed. She woke, chilled, in the night, and snuggled closer to Denis. What she wouldn't do now for the old pewter bed-warmer they had brought from France! And if only she had another chance to be up first in the cold dawn light to blow the fading embers of the cabin fire to flame with the hide bellows, she would never complain again.

In the morning, when they had eaten a meagre breakfast, Justine voiced an idea. "Denis, I think we'll try to see the ship arrive."

He looked overjoyed. "You mean we're going back home?"

"Oh, no. We'll go up on the ridge and watch it from there. No one will see us. They'll all be down at the wharf waiting for relatives and letters from home." She knew that Gervaise's family had been awaiting news for two years.

They set out after a noon meal, and the forest soon swallowed them from the village's view. Although there was no trail, the way was an easy one, carpeted with years of pine and spruce needles which made their journey mercifully quiet. The only sounds were the cries of the birds and the warnings of small animals as they scuttered across their path. They stopped halfway up the ridge to look down. "We're high enough," Justine decided. "We'll hide here."

"We could climb a tree," Denis suggested. "Then we could really see."

"And be seen," Justine reminded him. "Look here, there's a little knoll. We can lie behind it and peer over the top and see the whole village!"

They heard the wild shouts even before they caught sight of the billowing sails. They watched in silence as the sails were furled and the ship, accompanied by screaming gulls and a flotilla of Indian canoes, slipped into port. The entire village was gathered to welcome it, and even up on the hill they could hear the cries of rejoicing as the gangplank was lowered and the ship's passengers began to disembark. Some of them fell on their knees, kissing the soil in an ecstasy of thanksgiving, others sought familiar figures in the crowd and embraced them. But when Denis watched the long shapes of folded blankets being passed hand to hand from the deck, he asked, "What are those?"

"People who've been taken ill with fever or had their minds affected by the long journey from France." She knew it could take two months for the voyage. Their own had begun in mid-April and had not ended until the second week in June. Some had not survived that journey, and had been buried at sea.

"You don't remember when the bell came, do you, Denis?"

"The bell? Which bell?"

"The bell for the little stone church. It was made for us in France and came safely all the way. That was three years ago, when you were only five. There was a special festival with all the village feasting and dancing, and a special mass to Saint Anne, the patron saint of the Saguenay Indians. And Monsieur Benoît played his fiddle."

Denis gazed longingly down on the shifting scene. "Will there be feasting tonight, Justine?"

"Of course. The women will have made huge cauldrons of pea soup and dozens of pies filled with meat and gravy." Her mouth watered. "They may have even roasted a whole pig or a side of venison, because these travellers have had to live on hard biscuits and water for the last part of their journey."

"And will they have sweet cakes, Justine, like Gervaise brought us?"

"There'll be the cakes you like so much, sweetened with maple syrup. And the wild strawberries will be ripe; they'll have those, too. Perhaps there'll be cranberries crystallized in molasses and maybe the ship has brought some figs or oranges, or even cinnamon for the apple treats. And of course the Indians will make their own feast of welcome. They'll have elk and bear and sea lion and beaver."

"I wish I could be there. I just wish I could!"

"There'll be more ships coming, Denis." She put an arm around his thin shoulders. But would they be there to see them? How could she know? "This ship won't be here long. It's on its way upriver to Quebec and Montreal."

"Couldn't we go, too? That's far away from Monsieur Gaudin."

"No, that will have to be another day. Come along now. We daren't stay here too long. What do we want with their sweet cakes? We have one of our own left, and you shall have it."

In the haystack hideaway they tried to make the time pass quickly while they waited for dusk by playing counting games with some of the pebbles strewn at the entrance. Then Justine told stories of their own trip from the old country four years before. She described the excitement and the tears as they trundled all their belongings, provisions, furniture, implements and tools, and family souvenirs in a cart to the docks, the shouts of the crowds and the noise of the clogs on the cobbled streets, and then the sails streaming in wind and sun as they saw the brick-and-timbered walls of the little seaport fade in the distance. The cries of the relatives they would never see again faded, too, and their new life had begun. "Perhaps on the ship there will be letters from them and Gervaise will bring them, Denis. Wouldn't that be wonderful?"

But the early dusk came and went without Gervaise. "He can't get away from the celebrations. People would see him if he left. He'll come." She hugged her brother to her. "Just wait a while." And they waited, and still he did not come.

"Then tomorrow," Justine promised. "He'll be sure to be here tomorrow."

But he was not, even after a long tedious day of waiting. And then fear clutched at her heart. What had she condemned her brother to? What if Gervaise suspected that someone in the village knew of his doings? He would not come back, she knew that. He would trust her to act wisely on her own. What should she do?

Suddenly she knew. "Denis, we must leave this place. Someone may know we're here and that's why Gervaise hasn't come."

"Couldn't we go back, then? Somebody will look after us."

"No, there's no going back." Of that she was sure. On top of her fear of Monsieur Gaudin was now the fear of censure and punishment.

"Then what shall we do?" His pale little face was creased with anxiety.

"We'll leave this place and go on up the ridge. We'll find a hiding-place, and when Gervaise can come he'll find us there." She wished she felt the certainty her words carried. "If he hasn't come by daylight tomorrow morning, then before the sun is up, we'll leave."

"I'm hungry, Justine. Can't we eat some more?"

"Not now. We'll have to save what we have and eat it bit by bit."

"Monsieur Picard was a good man. If he hadn't gone up the river to Quebec he'd give us food."

And he might still at that, Justine thought suddenly. The idea had come with Denis's words. There might yet be food stored away in the cabin, undiscovered since Monsieur Picard's leaving. She would rise early on the following morning, while Denis was still asleep, and search. "Prayers now, and then sleep." She drew him to his knees. "Remember the Holy Mother is watching over us. We must be faithful, too." She trembled with the weight of the future and what it might bring, and with the decision she had made, which could end in disaster. But was such thinking "being faithful"? It was not. With an inward cry for help, she released her heart and hopes to heaven, drew the cloak over both of them, and slept.

CHAPTER FOUR

A Cave on the River

Sometime in the night she dreamed they were aboard ship in a terrible storm. Two people were swept overboard and she wakened with a start. Had she cried out? Then she knew why she had dreamed: outside, the air was loud with thunder. She crept to the edge of the stack to watch the lightning skipping along the ridge and crackling on the river. The huge clouds massed over her head rolled away and the morning star shone in a clear sky. Dawn was near. It was time to search the cabin. She knelt and said a prayer and then crept out into the half-light of early morning. The ground was wet and she trod carefully so as to leave no footprints.

The door of the cabin, hanging on broken leather thongs, stood open. As she groped her way inside, something blundered by her. A porcupine! She stood aside, respecting the sharp quills. She waited until her eyes became used to the dusk. Even in the dim light, she could see that the wilderness was reclaiming its own. Small trees had forced their way through the pine floor and through the flagstone hearth. Disorder showed the haste with which the Picard family had fled to safer places. There were two wooden chairs with rush seats half finished, a bolster covered with red calico that made a nest for a family of squirrels, and—saddest of all—the wooden cradle by the hearth, a reminder not only of a Picard baby who had died of the fever, but of Céleste and Nicolas. But there was no time for tears now. It was food she was looking for, and she found it in a bin, one of three lined up against the wall. Dried corncobs! What if the mice had been at them? Who cared? Then, hanging from the rafters, she saw dried fish and pumpkin. She climbed on a rickety wooden bench to fetch them down. In a cracked wooden bucket she found a handful of dried peas. She added these to the precious store in her cloak, which she had brought as a carrying-case. Then she took one last look about the cabin. In the growing light she saw the crude carved shelf beside the hearth and the rusted tin lamp upon it. But there was something else, a box. She moved quickly and brought it down. Opening it she found flint, steel, and a half-burnt cloth. A tinder box! She had found Monsieur Picard's tinder box, just like the one Papa had made sparks with to start fires. Now they could make a fire to cook food on! She fell on her knees. Oh, thank you! *Thank you, Holy Mother and Blessed Jesus, for bringing me here!*

Clutching the tinder box and the food in the cloak, she crept back to the haystack and wakened Denis. "Come, we mustn't waste any time. It's getting light."

"Where are we going?" He rubbed his eyes.

"Remember Bernard, the old trapper who found Michel when he was lost hunting and was so good to him? We'll try to find him. He'll help us."

"Where does he live?"

"In makeshift shelters along the ridge, wherever fancy takes him. Move quickly now. We must tidy the stack carefully so no one will suspect we've been here."

They found a narrow trail leading up over the sandy ridge through trembling aspen, jack pine, and white birch. Then the spruce, fir, and balsam began and grew denser as they moved on up, pausing every now and then to listen for suspicious sounds. When Denis stopped suddenly, she barged into him. "Listen! It's someone running!"

Her own heart thumped wildly and then she laughed. "It's a grouse, silly, beating its wings on a log." But they moved with increasing caution, listening for Iroquois and Monsieur Gaudin.

Halfway up the enormous hill they paused and glanced back. The village looked smaller now and they could see dim shapes hurrying to and from wells and stables. She felt safer. Only the odd hunter ventured up on the ridge, most often with hardy companions.

It was nearly midday by the time they had toiled their way to the top. Denis's small hands and face were scratched by brambles and low-hanging branches. "Can't we stop now?" he whimpered. "I'm too hungry and tired to go on."

"You had a piece of bread and some pie for breakfast. You mustn't worry about being hungry. We'll have to get used to it. But we'll stop here and eat some of the dried fish I found in the cabin."

"Dried? Without any cooking? Maman used to put it in soup!"

"Denis!" She tried to control her exasperation. "We have to eat what we have at hand. We'll have to eat many strange things just to stay alive." She looked straight into his eyes. "Now you have a choice. If you wish to go back to the village you can find Gervaise and his family. That way you'll have the good things of the village to eat. Or you can stay with me and put up with whatever food God sends us."

His answer was quick. "I'm not going back. I'll stay with you." He tried to look happy while he munched on the dried fish, and made an even greater effort to swallow it.

"Good for you." Justine hugged him. "When we've found a safe place we'll make a fire, and then we'll be able to cook."

They searched for signs of old Bernard, but found none. A fox loped by, a pair of rabbits bounded across their path, and a family of partridges ambled into view, but there was no Bernard.

Denis whirled at every sound. "Are there Indians here?"

"They're farther up the river." But they were hollow words. She did not know where the Indians were. But she knew what he was remembering: the day Thérèse and her brother were out berry-picking and disappeared, stolen by the Indians and perhaps adopted by them.

After they found the trail that wound in and out of the forest high on the ridge overlooking the river, she stopped now and then to look down. If only a lone trader would come into view, someone who had seen Bernard, or even had news of Michel. But the great River Saguenay, majestic and shimmering in the summer sun, was empty of human life.

In mid-afternoon Denis flopped on the forest floor. He was almost in tears. "Please, Justine, I'm trying to be brave, but I'm so tired. Do we have to go any farther?"

She looked down at him lovingly. "No. I think the village is far enough behind us now. We'll have a drink of water from Gervaise's flagon. Sparingly, mind, because we don't know where we'll get our next. Then we'll build a bough shelter for the night, a little at a time."

They found plenty of branches on the ground, broken from the treetops by high winds. They piled them one on the other to make a cone-shaped tipi. "Just like the Indians," Denis said.

"Yes, like the Montagnais. They live close by, you know."

"Are they fierce?" Denis drew close.

"No, they're our friends. You know the Indians who live around the chapel when the hunting season is over? They're Montagnais. Papa told me they act as middle-men in the fur trade."

"What does that mean?" Denis balanced a branch on his back.

"It means they get furs from the Algonkian tribes away to the north and they trade them to our fort at Tadoussac."

"Did Papa know the Montagnais who live up here?"

"He may have. Some of the ones who traded with him were special friends."

Exhausted with the long climb and the heat of the day, they lay down early inside their shelter of boughs. At first the mosquitoes hummed around their heads but they swatted as many as they could with petticoat and cloak and then, lulled by the evening mewing of gulls between the river shores, they slept.

It was still dark when he wakened her. He whispered, "I heard a cry. What could it be?"

She sat up. "A cry? Just wild animals in the night, I think." But when it came again, she was not at all sure. Could there be Iroquois nearby? When it came a third time it sounded weaker, farther away. She cuddled Denis in her arms and they both slept.

They wakened to a world of green light with the sun shining through the spruce boughs. The morning glistened with summer as they came out into it. "We'll have to find water today," Justine said. "Ours is nearly all gone."

After breakfast they went silently, stealthily, aware that eyes could be watching them from the depths of the forest. The silence was at times unearthly and frightening and even the reedy call of a red-winged blackbird was welcome on the lonely path.

Justine stopped suddenly. "Listen, I think I hear frogs. That could mean a pond."

But what direction the sound came from, they could not tell.

They had been an hour stalking through the forest when Justine fell. Denis rushed to her side. "Are you hurt? Oh, Justine, please don't be hurt!"

She sat up. "I'm not at all hurt. I fell over something." She stood up and looked down, then bent swiftly. She held in her hand a strange round wooden ball carved to look as if held by a human hand.

Denis eyed it warily. "What's that?"

Fear made her heart pound.

"A broken war club. Look, here's the handle." A few feet away lay a haft with carving on it. "It's probably been here for months. It can't harm us." But the thing spoke to her of Iroquois, of terror and raids in the night.

Later, when they found a necklet of shells broken and strewn on the ground, she knew. "Denis," she said, "there's been a raid here. Warriors bring these necklets with them on war parties as a kind of charm."

"Is it Iroquois? What shall we do?" He began to cry, muffling his sobs against her boy's jerkin.

"There now, Mousekin. We'll listen as silently as two owls, and if we hear nothing we'll go on, in God's loving care." As she spoke she tried to stifle the quiver of fear and doubt that made her own lips tremble.

An hour later they found a leather bag filled with roasted corn mixed with maple sugar. "Now we know it was a raid," she said solemnly.

"How do we know?"

"The Iroquois bring these bags filled with corn and maple sugar to eat when they're on raids far from their villages."

He looked like one of the animals they had startled on the forest path. "Then we should run, and fast!"

"Oh, no, we'll go on very carefully. They'll probably be leagues away by now." As if to bolster her faith, they found a tiny shrine in half-an-hour, in a close-thicketed grove of trees where they had crept to eat. There was a little statue of the Blessed Virgin and the Baby Jesus, crudely carved from wood and set against an enormous spruce. Sprays of faded wildflowers lay in front of it. "A shrine!" she whispered. "Some *coureur de bois* made this and knelt here to give thanks for a safe journey! Let's do the same." She knelt quickly and pulled Denis down beside her. It was a sign, she knew, that loving presences were watching over them. All she had to do was move carefully and wait for answers.

They came upon what remained of the Indian village half an hour later, when they broke through the forest into a clearing. Only one conical lodge of birchbark remained standing; the rest had been burned to the ground. The scent of smoke and terror still hung in the quiet air.

Denis looked up at her fearfully. "What happened?"

She still spoke in a whisper, knowing that danger could be lurking. "It was a Montagnais village. The Iroquois have destroyed it."

"Will they come back?"

"Not if people died here. They'll believe the place is haunted by the spirits of the dead." It was what she hoped, what she wanted to believe.

"Where are all the dead people, then?" Denis cowered behind her. "I don't want to see them!"

"They've been taken away, perhaps at night, in the dark, by those who survived." But she dared not look up. She knew that sometimes the Indians lodged their dead in the tree branches awaiting burial. She began to move forward cautiously, Denis at her heels, weaving her way through broken moosehide shields, smashed bows and arrows, crumpled and burned moccasins and breechcloths, and caribou bones. Scorched animal skins that had served as blankets lay close to the ring of stones in the centre of the encampment, where the communal fire for cooking had been laid. From the fire itself she bent to pick up some seal meat, almost black with roasting, and added it to her meagre store in the bag.

When she swooped to the ground a moment later Denis thought she was hiding and joined her. She was triumphant. "Look, Denis, a clay pot! It's a bit broken but it's still good enough for cooking in! And here's another one!"

Denis smiled. "Then maybe we won't have to eat raw fish all dried up!"

"Maybe. We'll have to find a place where we can make a fire without it being seen." She stared around at the village barricade of trees that had been burned to stumps. "Denis, if Indians lived here there must be water close by. We have to have water. We'll explore carefully and listen."

A few moments later they were rewarded by the gentle splash of a waterfall. The sound grew louder as they quickened their pace and broke through a thicket of firs. A beautiful sight met their eyes. A stream glided gently at their feet, singing merrily over richly coloured pebbles and stones, glittering in the late morning light. They cupped the water in their hands and drank their fill, then bathed their faces until they shone.

Suddenly there was a loud smack across the water. They jumped at the sound. Justine pointed. "It's only a beaver, Denis, below the waterfall. He's making a home and damming up the river." She felt as if she had found a friend going about his homely, natural business in a world of terror. "We mustn't stop to watch him. We must find a place where it's safe to spend the night."

They ate sparingly from the bag first, chewing on the dry, hard corncobs they had found in the cabin and washing them down with water from the stream. When they returned to the trail that overlooked the river, Justine turned around to warn Denis to step carefully so near the cliff face. He was not there. Her heart leaped wildly. He had fallen! Denis had fallen down the precipice and been killed!

"Denis! Denis, where are you?"

"I'm here, Justine! Berries are growing in the cracks down there. I'm going to get them!"

She peered down. "Don't! Stay where you are!"

But he was already slithering down the rocky slope like a mountain goat. Suddenly his foot slipped. She cried out in fear, unable to check herself. "Denis!"

"I'm all right, there's a ledge here. I landed on it." His voice was shaky, uncertain. "I won't fall into the river."

"Come up! Come up at once!" She was trembling from head to foot. She tried to calm herself. "Can you find a way?"

There was no answer. He had fallen then! He was tumbling down through the massive boulders to the greedy waters below! And it was all her fault because she had run away.

"Justine!"

He was there, still there! Oh, praise God! He was still alive!

His voice came again, muffled and strange. "Justine, there's a hole here!"

"A hole? What do you mean, a hole?"

"A hole in the rock. It goes in, way in."

She felt like screaming her warning. "Don't you go in! There could be a bear in there, or worse!"

"I could just get inside and see what it's like."

"No, Denis! I'm coming down!" The way she found was almost the one down which he had fallen, but there were toeholds in the rock wall, and shrubs, trees, and berry bushes growing on its face in the crevices. When she reached the massive shelf she hugged him to her with tears streaming down her face. "Oh, don't do that again, Mousekin, don't do it!"

He looked up at her, astonished. "But I didn't do anything. I just slipped. I'm all right, and look what I found!"

It was a cave, there was no doubt of that. She got down on her knees and peered within. "I can't see anything in there. I think we'll take a chance and go in."

She looked about her first. Mosses, lichens, and wild-flowers clung to the boulders at the cave entrance. There were birds' nests on the ledge itself and one hanging inside. With a wild cry its owner fled past them, and as they crouched and entered, three more forms swooped around them and out into the air, making them bend quickly to the cave floor. "Bats," Justine said. "But if *we* want to live here, *they'll* have to move."

Denis straightened and looked at her wonderingly. "You mean we could *live* here?"

"For now. Why not? We'd be safe from view, and we could rest here until we know what we can do."

"The wild animals wouldn't come down and find us, would they?"

"No, not down here. I was trying to scare you with the bear. It's too hard for them to get down, and I think we'll be safe from people, too." Not Monsieur Gaudin now, but the Iroquois, if they should return. But she did not say it.

"Where shall we get things to eat, then?"

"We can eat plants and berries, the way the Indians do, and maybe we can catch some fish. There must be a lot in that river." She began to move about the dark interior. "And we'll build a fire at the opening of the cave to cook our food in the clay pots. If we keep the smoke down no one will see it."

They looked about them, relishing the damp coolness of the cave after the July heat on the forest floor. Two salamanders disappeared into a crack, a spider with long legs spun a web over their heads, and little brown and yellow cave crickets chirruped at their feet. Somehow these natural citizens of the cave going about their daily living made her feel safer. She ventured farther into the dark interior. "Look here, Denis." She pointed to massive slabs of rock that had settled where parts of the cave roof had fallen in, perhaps years ago. "We can use these for a table and for a place to sleep. There's even a shelf high up where I can hide my girl's clothes!"

"What's this, Justine?" Denis held out something he had found on the cave floor.

"A turtle shell." Justine turned it over in her hands. "We'll keep it. We might even use it for something."

"How would a turtle get in here?"

"Perhaps it fell through before the cracks in the roof were overgrown with plants and trees, and then the insects and things ate it up."

"Unlucky old turtle!"

"Yes, but lucky us." And she did feel lucky. This would give them a chance to breathe, to rest a while and consider what to do next. "Denis, we'll build a shrine at the edge of the stone platform over here and pray our thanks for finding this place."

They made a little cross of branches and propped it up between the rocks and placed before it green moss, pink wildflowers, and red berries. Then they gave thanks, kneeling and crossing themselves. It was just as they rose that Justine saw the painting. "Denis, what's this?"

He moved with her farther down the cave to the end wall. "It's a picture, Justine! Somebody's been down here making a drawing!"

"Of a caribou." It was a kind of stick painting, crudely but powerfully drawn, showing the caribou leaping in flight, and the red of the ochre it was done with glowed in the half-light.

"Who did it?" Denis looked puzzled.

"Some traveller who found shelter down here in a storm, Denis." But she knew it was not just any traveller; it was an Indian who had done the painting. So the Indians had found this place and sheltered here, perhaps from an ancient enemy, or to weather out a storm. Whatever the reason, she said nothing to Denis, even when she found the remains of a broken bone tool lodged up against the cave wall. Her own heart was filled with anxiety. She would not burden her brother with more fears than he could stand.

"Let's build a fire," she said purposefully, "just at the entrance to the cave."

"I can go and bring some boughs."

"No, Denis, green boughs make smoke and that means someone would see it. We'll go up together and find some dry kindling. That makes an almost smoke-free fire. Don't you remember the hearth at home?" The hearth at home. How far away and long ago it seemed now. But they had survived. Remembering, she crossed herself. They would go on surviving.

Beckoning to Denis, she led the way up the cliff face.

Later, in a haste of hunger, they ate some of the contents of Monsieur Picard's bin that they had cooked over the fire, relishing the hot food. Denis went in to fall quickly asleep on the stone bed, and Justine covered him with her cloak. She was not long following, exhausted as she was with anxiety and responsibility, and the long trek.

When the hard rock bit into her bones she did not care. They seemed safe at the moment and tomorrow they would bring down some pine branches to make a softer bed. She was asleep in a moment.

When she wakened she did not know for an instant where she was—the dark of the cave pressed in on her, and she trembled. Then she remembered and was glad. But what had roused her from sleep? She knew when it came again, the same cry they had heard before in the night. What was it? It seemed close now. She crept out to the shelf and listened. It was as if all the dark beyond the cave were breathing, like a monstrous wild animal ready to pounce. She looked down at the vast river shining below in the moonlight. It snaked away north into the wilderness like the giant serpent Grandmother had described in a folk tale far away in France. But there seemed to be not a creature stirring. Then the cry came again, this time weaker. Was it Iroquois? Had they come back? She knew they seldom raided here, choosing to attack the larger settlements of Quebec, Montreal, and Trois Rivières, closer to their own territory. Shivering, she retreated to the cave. She lay down again beside Denis, put her arms around him, and once more fell asleep.

CHAPTER FIVE

The Boy Is Dying!

"Do you think we could ever see way up there in the wilderness where Michel has gone?" Denis stood on the ledge the next morning while Justine cooked breakfast.

She came to stand beside him, gazing upriver to the far reaches of the Saguenay, which wound bold and majestic between immense hills. "Not that far, Denis, although it almost seems as if we could. The wilderness goes on for ever. Come and eat now. Then we'll go back to the Montagnais village to see if there's anything we can use."

"Do we have to?"

She knew what he meant. It was a place of death and it made her shudder, but life and survival were at stake. "Yes, we have to, after we've eaten."

They had a bath first in the crystal-clear water of the stream, while the beaver went about his business of building a lodge, accepting them as part of his environment. The water was ice cold but they tried not to shout as it washed over them. Then Justine shook out their clothing and they dressed, refreshed and somehow heartened.

But the burned village brought them back to reality. They crept among its sad remains, eyes intent on the ground. They came upon scorched, half-made snow-shoes, a torn but still decorated medicine-bag, and the remnant of a burned vest, intricately embroidered with quills and beads. "See the glass beads, Denis?" She spoke low, conscious of ears in the forest. "These show this village traded with us, perhaps even with Papa in his fort store."

"How do you know that?"

"Because of the beads. Before we came they used to sew just seeds and porcupine quills and shells on their clothing. The beads are what we trade with them in exchange for animal skins. Papa had some behind his counter."

"Did the Indians who were burned know Papa, then?"

"Probably. The Montagnais often brought him furs to trade." How strange, she thought, that all their lives should have been altered by fire, and in some cases destroyed. Whispering, she said a quick prayer for the Montagnais who had perished or fled.

Searching steadily, they gathered up spear points, bone awls, and a large stretch of caribou hide, all left behind in the necessity of flight.

"Why did the Iroquois burn the village?" Denis asked. "They're all Indians."

"Yes, but different tribes. The English side with the Iroquois and our French traders with the Algonkian and Montagnais, and they're all battling one another for the best fur-trading routes in the north."

"Where do the Iroquois come from, then?"

"From south of the St. Lawrence River." How would she ever see them if they came again, flitting like ghosts from tree to tree?

Denis reached out and clutched her arm. "Will they burn our village?"

"Our" village? Would it ever be their village again?
"Perhaps not. Come along now, keep searching. Anything we find here could help us."

They had given up hope of finding more when she saw something shining under a heap of smashed clay. She dove to the ground. "Denis! Denis, look what I've found."

He turned to stare. "A knife!" And beside it lay a sheath of caribou hide adorned with beads and quills in a floral design.

"Yes, a knife! The handle is broken but the blade is still sharp. Oh, Denis, we can do so many things with this!" She held it aloft triumphantly. "And the first thing we'll do is cut some wild plant shoots like Maman used to have us gather for soup or to boil as vegetables. I've seen burdock and blackberry, chicory and bulrushes. We can use them all!" But most of all, she thought, we can use this wonderful knife that probably came from Papa's own trading counter, given over for a load of animal skins!

Compared to recent meals their supper was a feast, but still Denis was hungry. "It's like a fast-day meal at home, Justine. I don't ever feel filled up."

She recalled with a pang the fast-day meals of onions and slices of wholemeal bread on Fridays and Saturdays. If only she could have those now, she would never grumble again. "Denis, we're so lucky to have food. It's summer and the forest is full of things we can eat. We don't have to eat bark and moss like the *coureurs de bois* to keep from starving."

"Is that all Michel has to eat?"

"I don't know what Michel eats." If only Denis would stop asking questions. And how she wished she knew where Michel was. But she tried to keep, deep in her heart, the faith that he was still alive.

As the dark came down over the river, Denis sat watching the stars, and the gulls wheeling and mewing. "Justine, you know you said the Iroquois were afraid of the ghosts of the dead people in the village. Will the ghosts come for us?"

"Why should they come for us? We've done them no harm." She remembered the quiet prayer she had said for them. "Come, we'll pray for them before our shrine and that will bless them, and us, too."

She wakened again uneasily in the night, wondering if a cry had startled her, the cry that had no answer, but there was only the far-off hooting of an owl in the forest above and the timid rustle of small creatures inside and outside the cave.

It was the flapping of a bat's wings that brought her awake in the morning. She laughed down at Denis as the creature swooped past them. "He doesn't like to share with us, Denis, but the crickets don't mind. I heard them singing in the night." Just as they used to sing at home, she remembered, around the fire. But this was home now. "Get up, lazybones. Today we'll bathe again and then catch some fish."

She was in the stream, barefoot, wading out towards the middle and trying to catch at the shoals of fish swimming by, when she saw that Denis had gone. Panic seized her. She searched along the edge of the forest, stricken with fear. Where could he be? She couldn't cry out because she didn't know what lay beyond, in the darkness of spruce and pine. And then suddenly there he was, standing as though entranced, between the trunks of two massive fir trees. She ran to him. "Denis! Why did you do that? You must stay near me if we're to live!" She hugged him to her, and then she felt him trembling from head to foot. His face was ashen and he could hardly speak. "What's the matter? Tell me quickly! What have you seen?"

His voice came in a whisper: "An Indian."

At once she imagined the forest staring at them with a hundred eyes. "An Indian? Where?" Where there was one, there would be more.

He tried to find shelter in her arms. "I'm scared, Justine. I don't want to see him again."

"Then tell me where you saw him, or how are we to get away?" She could have shaken him in her urgency but instead she held him close. "Tell me, Denis!"

"He's back there." He pointed through the trees. "I saw some berries that way yesterday and I went to find them."

"And was he hiding behind a tree? Didn't he come after you?"

"He couldn't. He was on the ground!"

"Dead, you mean?" *Oh, praise God and forgive me!* If the Indian was dead they needn't fear him.

"A Montagnais, then. One of those killed in the burning of the village." She felt a sudden relief. But why had he been left?

He drew away from her and looked up, puzzled. "But he wouldn't be a warrior. He's only a boy."

"A boy like you?"

"I think he's a little older than I am. He's bigger, almost as big as you, but I didn't stay to see because he's all tied down and I was frightened."

"Tied down? Denis, what is this? Try to be calm and tell me exactly what you saw."

"Well, when I was looking for the berries I came to a big clear space and in the middle there was this Indian boy tied down like this." He flung his arms and legs wide to indicate a spread-eagled position.

"Were there ropes around his feet and legs?"

"I don't know. I didn't stay to see. I just ran to you."

She pulled him beside her behind a clump of wild shrubs that hugged the stream. "We must think what to do now."

"Why did they kill him like that? He's only a boy."

"Yes, and the Indians are always good to children, even those who don't belong to their own tribe. This must have been an act of vengeance, Denis."

"But he's only a boy," Denis repeated. "Just like me!"

"Perhaps the Montagnais killed an Iroquois boy, maybe even the son of their chief in a raid, and the Iroquois came back to take revenge. Someday the Montagnais may come back to look for him."

"But the animals will have eaten him."

She took his hands in her own. "We can't leave him there, Denis. We must go and bury him."

"But I don't want to. Please don't make me!"

"Would you leave him there to be devoured by wild animals? Of course you wouldn't. We'll set his body free, say prayers for him, and give him a proper burial."

Denis said nothing.

"Denis, if we're to live until we find someone to shelter us and to love us, if we're to live until Michel comes home, we have to be brave. This Indian is dead, God keep his soul. He can do us no harm." She recalled suddenly the cries they had heard in the night. Now she knew who had made them. Her whole body ached at the thought of the boy lying there in the night with no one to rescue him.

"I'll go then." Denis stood up. "Can we do it all very fast and get it over with?"

"As fast as we can. Lead the way."

Denis hung back. "There's something else."

"What's that?"

"He doesn't have any clothes on."

"What does that matter to me, silly? Don't you think I've seen nakedness before now? Who bathed you and

dressed you until you grew old enough to do it yourself?
Indians sometimes wear little clothing except a breech-
cloth, and the younger ones wear nothing in summer.
Come along now, let's not waste any more time."

He set off reluctantly and she followed him, treading
with caution. He paused a few feet from a glade of trees.
Beyond that there was a natural clearing. "He's in there,"
he whispered. "*You* look!"

She looked and her heart cried out. The boy appeared
to be about ten or eleven. His brown body was tied to
the ground, hide thongs at wrist and ankle. The sun beat
down mercilessly on the rock, the forest floor, and the
body. He must have died of thirst, if he had not died of
hunger. She glanced warily around the clearing to make
sure they were alone. Then she took Denis's hand and
crept towards the silent form.

"Kneel beside me. We must pray for him." She withdrew the ruby red necklace from her shirt and clutched it
tightly. "Oh, Blessed Jesus, Holy Mary, Mother of God,
this is your child, too. Keep him safe with you and watch
over his soul." She crossed herself.

"Justine!" Denis tugged at her sleeve.

"Shh. We must pray and then make haste to move
him."

"But his eyelids! It's his eyelids!"

"What about them? They're burned with the hot sun."

"They moved!"

"Moved? You saw them move?"

"Yes! Yes, I know I did. As if he was trying to see. It
was just for a second, while you were praying!"

"Denis, he may be alive! I left the flagon by the
stream. Go fetch it quickly. It's filled with fresh water."

He was back in an instant holding it out to her. "What
shall we do?"

"I want you to hold his lips open for me. I'm going to
try to make him drink."

"But I don't want to touch him!"

"Shame on you!" she blazed forth in anger. "The boy is dying! Don't you want him to live? What if it were you lying there? Do as I say at once!"

He looked at her in fright and then bent to do her bidding. As she leaned towards the Indian boy his eyes opened once more. They were glazed with his semi-conscious state, and yet filled with resigned terror, like those of a wild animal caught in a trap. Then they closed again and Justine wet his lips and took the edge of her jerkin to bathe his face with cold water.

"This won't do, Denis. We must cut him free and take him back to the cave, where we can tend him properly."

"How can we do that?"

"By carrying him in my old cloak. But first we have to cut these thongs. I'm so glad we have this knife!" She drew it from her belt and cut the ties in a moment. She gently rubbed the boy's wrists and ankles, chafed by the harsh thongs, but he did not stir.

"Shall I fetch the cloak?"

"No, I'm faster than you. You stay here with him until I get back."

One look at her told him he must not protest. She ran swiftly to the cliff and down the face to the cave, breathless with the need for haste. When she came back Denis had not moved and neither had the other boy.

There was another wild look from those dark eyes as Justine and Denis wrapped him in the cloak and with great difficulty carried him along to the cave descent. But he made no movement; his body was limp and heavy in the cloak.

When they came to the cliff edge they lowered him to the ground. "We'll have to carry him by his head and feet. It's too steep to hold the cloak. Be careful now!"

Somehow they got him into the cave and onto the shale floor. They sat back and rested, breathing deeply.

Still the boy did not move or open his eyes. "Where shall we put him, Justine?"

"We could try the rock slab we use for our table. We'll move the spruce boughs from my bed. We can always fetch more of them. Then I'll cover the boughs with my old petticoat so the needles don't dig into his body. We'll have to check the boy for fleas and sponge them off."

In due course all was done and they sat beside the rock slab gazing up at him. "In a minute," Justine said, "you hold his mouth open again and I'll dribble more water in. He must have water."

"Can't he have anything to eat?"

"Not for some time. The water will keep him alive."

They maintained their vigil until night came, stopping only for a hasty meal of dried fish and berries. Then Justine covered the boy with her cloak and went to sit on the ledge, exhausted and afraid. *If only Gervaise were here, he would know what to do.*

Denis sat beside her. "Justine, do you think he's one of the Montagnais Papa knew?"

She smiled and patted his shoulder. "Perhaps he is. He may have come to the fort when his father traded furs. It's good to know Papa may have known him and we've rescued him. Papa would be glad."

There was a moment's silence before Denis spoke again. "Justine, remember Star Boy? I only saw him twice at the fort when I went with Papa. But this boy looks like him."

She turned to him in surprised approval. "Yes, he does! He's a little older but he *does* look like Star Boy!" How could she forget Papa's tales of Star Boy? He had been the son of a Montagnais chief who traded at the fort, Papa's friend. He had been born at a time when the light of the moon was totally eclipsed by the earth's shadow. A single silver star had shone in the April evening sky, a lamp of hope to the Indians in the fearful darkness. So Star Boy he had become, his merry ways making him a great favourite of Papa's. But the fever had taken him in two days. Papa had come home from the fort to tell them, his eyes filled with tears. And now Papa himself had gone.

She remembered him with deep sadness as they sat gazing down the river. The far lonely cry of a loon echoed her sadness and then, quite suddenly, came a howl that ricocheted along the ridge and out over the canyon. Denis stiffened. "What's that?"

"A wolf." She drew him close. "You know they live up here in the forest. We'll just keep out of its way. Wait here and I'll take a look at our little friend again."

When she came back Denis was slumped with his head between his knees. "What's the matter?"

"Justine, shall we all die now? I don't want to die!"

"But we're not going to die! We've found this fine home and we can stay hidden as long as we wish. You know we can find food in the forest."

"But don't you think the Iroquois will come back to see if the Indian boy is dead?"

"They'd think there was nothing left to look for, Denis. They'd think a bear or wolf had done away with him. No, we're safe here, I know it." And how she wished she believed her own words! Because now there were two for her to look after instead of one, and she was responsible for all their decisions.

"Do you think we'll have to stay here for ever, Justine?" His eyes in the half-light glistened with tears.

"Of course not, Mousekin. We'll find Bernard, or Michel will come home, and all will be well." She looked up at the night sky. "I can remember when just to sit on a ledge outside a cave and watch the stars would have seemed like paradise."

"When?"

"Aboard the sailing ship coming from France. You were too small to remember the storms and the icebergs and the terrible way a hundred of us were all jammed in the hold. The gales blew and the sails tipped over almost to touch the waves and we could hardly breathe with the stench of illness all around us. When the waves were like mountains we had to find a space to lie flat to eat, holding on to our wooden platters with both hands so they didn't go flying through the air. At least here we have our own stew-pot, cracked though it is, and the peace to eat and sleep."

"Yes, but I'm hungry again, Justine."

"We'll eat tomorrow. Remember we have three to share food now."

"Will you sing me a lullaby then?"

"I will, and you'll be asleep in a minute." She tucked him in with her hempen skirt. The Indian had not stirred, but she felt his breath with her hand. She knelt to say prayers and ask for blessings. Then, laying a hand on each still form, she sang a lullaby softly until Denis was deeply asleep.

She stood gazing down in the dusk at the motionless body of the Indian boy. Her heart ached with sympathy for what he must have suffered. But they had come in time, praise God for that! Bending to give a swift soft touch to his forehead, she went out to the ledge again, to think over the events of the day. The image of the Indian boy tied down in the forest, defenceless, had burned itself into her memory. She knew she would never forget it. Who would ever do such a thing, and to a child? It must have been another Indian with great hate in his heart, she was sure of that. And yet she had heard that the English and French inflicted cruelties too. After all, what had Monsieur Gaudin had in mind for her?

She recalled the night a newcomer had joined them at the supper table in the cabin. He was Guillaume, an old friend of Papa's, fresh from France. A philosopher, Papa had called him, and when she asked what that meant, he said, "One who searches for the meaning of life, little one. He is good for us. Here in the New World we have no time for such wonderings. We're too busy trying to stay alive. Guillaume has come to study life in the colony and to write a tract about it when he goes home to France."

As she stood at the lip of the ledge gazing at the vast canopy of stars and their reflection in the mighty river waters below, she wished she had Guillaume beside her to tell her something of his thoughts about why things happened the way they did. She remembered his arrival at the cabin and the discussion that followed. At first his voice had been low and soft, a poet's voice. But then suddenly he had thundered, "And why have we brought the wars here to the New World? Is it not enough that we torture and pillage and plunder in the old lands, without bringing our grievances and our enmities here?" At that he had struck the table so that all the pewter dishes rattled. "These Indians are innocent children of nature. It is the English and French who have brought war between Iroquois and Algonkian, with their greed for furs and the wealth to be made from them. If it weren't for the foppish European fashion of dressing in skins and beaver hats, there would be no need for battles over the best fur-trade routes."

Then Papa had confessed that he had been ashamed of some of the French fur traders when he'd seen them at the great fur fair in Montreal, trying to make the Indians drunk so they could cheat them. She knew that had never happened at the fort with Papa behind the counter. He welcomed the fur brigades when they came home in the late fall from the wilderness, and the occasional lone Montagnais with skins to barter.

Guillaume had worn no fur. He had come flapping in at the door like a huge bird, his ragged black wool cape swirling about his thin body and, shadowing his deep-set, sparkling eyes, a great broad-brimmed black hat frayed at the edges, as were all his clothes.

"Guillaume." Papa's voice was calm but firm. "You must know there was warfare among the tribes long before the fur traders came. True, our rivalries have undoubtedly made it worse, but it was the fur trade that opened up our New World for settlement, don't forget that."

But Guillaume didn't want to believe any good of the fur trade. To him, it was the English and the French who pitted one tribe against another, and those in the settlements, Indian or French, were the ones who suffered.

Did this mean that the young Montagnais lying wasted and asleep in the cave had been pinned to the ground so cruelly because of the fur wars? And all his suffering was caused by the fashions far away in the old country? What could she do about it? Only care for him, she thought. Make him one of them and hope they all lived. She knelt down and prayed to the Blessed Virgin for guidance. As she prayed, the moon came slowly up over the dark forest and laid a radiant path on the waters far below. It was a sign, and she would accept it. There would be light on her own path.

CHAPTER SIX

A Fall Down the Cliff

"What are you doing with the knife?"

"Making him a breechcloth from the caribou hide we found in the ruins. Don't be noisy. I don't want him wakened. He needs rest."

It was still dusky in the cave while they whispered. As she slit the hide to make a thong girdle to circle the boy's waist, the rays of the early-morning sun sought the cave interior and outlined the still form beneath the cloak.

She moved closer and touched him. There was no response on the small face. Denis had been right, she thought. He would be of an age between the two of them. He was fine-boned and wiry, with black hair longer than her own boyish cut, almost to his shoulders.

Denis came to stand beside her. "Does he have to stay here?"

"Where can he go? His family and the other Montagnais have flown. If he knew where they'd gone he could follow them, but they could be leagues and leagues away by now."

"We don't know his name. What shall we call him?" But before she had a chance to answer he spoke again, hesitatingly. "Could we call him Star Boy?"

She knew he was trying to reassure himself about this stranger in their midst, about everything. "Denis, that's the very answer! We'll call him Star Boy!" And this one, she thought suddenly, fiercely, will live.

"How shall we talk to him? He won't be able to speak French and we can't speak Montagnais."

"I know, but when he wakes up I'll talk to him as if he understands every word."

Denis looked at her doubtfully. "Then I think you can start now. His eyes just opened."

She knelt by the boy's side and stretched out her hands. Her voice rose and fell with the rhythms of speech as if she would weave a net of her words to draw him to her. "Star Boy, we're your friends. Our God in Heaven and the Holy Mother and the Blessed Jesus are yours, too. We're all their children. We want you to be one of us. We want you to live with us and share the food we have and our safety in the cave. We'll do you no harm. Please don't be afraid. We must face the wilderness together. Like you, we've lost all we had." She moved closer to him, willing him to keep his eyes on her face.

But he lay silent, staring at her wide-eyed and watchful. Why, oh why, hadn't she learned some of the Montagnais language? Papa had had to do that to deal with the Indian traders. But that had been at the fort. She'd had nothing to do with them. Her days and many of her nights had been taken up helping Maman with the two babies and the concerns of house and farm, and try-ing to school Denis, when she could catch him. A smile and a gesture had been her only means of greeting the Montagnais on the rare occasions she was allowed to go to the fort with Papa. But she would go on trying to make Star Boy understand. She had to.

"Denis, bring the corn from the fire. I'll mash it with water and the dried fish and try to feed him."

But when she approached, the Indian boy tried to struggle up. Then his weakness overcame him and he fell back, his face turned to the cave wall.

They watched over him all day, Justine yearning to make him respond. On the second day he seemed, oddly, to be stronger. She could see his muscles tense as she came near with food and water, but now that he was conscious he would take neither. When they needed fresh water one of them stayed beside him while the other went on the errand.

On the third morning when they woke, he was gone. Justine could not believe it. She felt as bereft as if she had lost a friend. How could he have found the strength if he had eaten nothing? She discovered the answer when she went to her cache of food at the rear of the cave. She had thought on the previous day that there had not been as much there as she had counted on. Now she knew why. He had been up in the silence and the darkness while they slept, eating from their store. But he had not taken it all. There was still some dried pumpkin and a little seal meat.

When they had eaten they went up on the ridge to search for him but the task seemed hopeless. "Has he gone to find his family, do you think?" Denis asked.

"I don't know. Perhaps. We can't risk calling out. But we'll go and wait by the stream. He may come there to drink."

Hidden by a clump of trees, they watched all morning, but there was no sign of him. The beaver was hard at work again on his lodge and Justine thought wryly that he was really the cause of all the tribal warfare and the enmity between French and Iroquois. Poor innocent little animal going about his business, unaware that a trapper might soon be after him.

To her shock, a trapper did pass in mid-afternoon as they were again keeping watch. He was a big, burly fellow, a stranger. Perhaps he was from a village farther up the river. Justine did not dare to call out or approach him, for he would want to take them back to the village. That she must avoid at all costs.

They watched him follow the course of the river and then crept away quietly to the cliff edge.

"Justine, there's a canoe down there!"

"Where?"

"Tied up at a tree! It's right below us!"

"It's the trapper's canoe. He's carried his traps here and come up the cliff."

"But why can't we go down and take the canoe? He hasn't seen us."

"Where would we go? Up the Saguenay is only wilderness, no settlements at all. We would die there."

"We could go back to our village." He eyed her, his whole face shining with hope.

"No, Denis." Nothing had changed that resolve. "I shall never go back while Monsieur Gaudin is there. Never!" Never was a long time. She felt despairing, despairing of rescue, despairing of the Indian boy they had found and lost again. She tried to hide her tears.

"Why are you crying?" Denis reached for her hand and held it tightly. "Don't cry. I'll be brave. I won't ever leave you, and I won't ask about going home again."

"Of course you won't, Denis." She hugged him to her in a swift movement. "We'll be all right, wait and see. I'm just troubled about Star Boy."

"I don't think you need be." Denis sounded content. "I think he's gone back to his own people. It's better for him."

"But he wouldn't know where they went. I don't want to think of him alone in the forest, trying to find his family." She drew Denis away from the cliff. "Still, we have to get on with our own business. We're nearly out of food. Let's try to make a net to catch some fish. There are plenty in the stream."

They ate supper first, making a mush of what was left of the spoils from Monsieur Picard's cabin. "I'm still hungry," Denis said after. "Is that all there is?"

"That's all. Now come and help me gather branches to make a net."

But their efforts were useless. The pliable stalks they found to use as rope to tie the branches together slithered away at their touch and would not make a bond. "We'll work at it again tomorrow." She tried to hide her loss of hope. "Come and sit on the ledge and I'll tell you another tale of King Dagobert."

Later, with Denis asleep curled up on her arm, she wondered what was to become of them. For Denis's sake should she make her way back to the village and take what came? What about Star Boy alone in the forest? Would he live, or die alone, killed by an Iroquois or by some ferocious wild beast?

She slept late. When she wakened the sun was shining in the cave and Denis was out on the ledge. He called softly, "Justine, come here! I think there's something coming down the river!"

She sprang to his side. "Two canoes! Coming home from the fur hunt, Denis! They may be from our own village! Come on! Let's get down to the river shore and hide until we can see who it is."

They clambered quickly to the cliff edge and found the path that the trapper the day before had used. On the riverbank they hid by the lapping water, behind a clump of black spruce. "Denis!" She kept her voice low. "I think it's Pierre Clermont and his brothers. Do you remember how he set off last spring and we all went down to the dock to see him off?"

"He was Papa's friend. But how do you know it's him from so far away?"

"Don't you remember? He always flies the flag of France on the prow of his canoe, and there it is!"

Denis looked jubilant. "If he sees us, he'll come for us and he'll know what to do! He'll help us!"

"I know he will! Shout as loud as you can, Denis. Wave your arms. Take off your jerkin and wave that, too!"

They screamed until it seemed impossible that they would not be heard. Their voices rebounded from the massive cliffs all around them, but they did not reach across the wide waters of the Saguenay.

"I can hear them singing! Why can't they hear us?" Denis was in tears.

"It's the way the wind's blowing. Our voices are being blown away!" She tried to sound cheerful. "Never mind. If Pierre Clermont has come home, more homeward-bound traders from our village may come along. We'll have to keep watch each morning. Somebody will hear us." But her heart sank as she watched the canoes fade from sight and as the voices of the men, singing in unison to the dipping of their paddles in the river water, faded too. She imagined the welcome that awaited Pierre from his wife and children in the village. What a feast there would be! What singing and dancing! "Come along," she said trying to hide her sadness. "We'll gather bark and berries to eat. And we'll look for mushrooms and plants too."

She began to clamber up the cliff path, Denis ahead of her and clearly in her sight. Suddenly, as she searched for the toehold he had used, he gave a frantic scream and slithered down the cliff into her arms. "What happened?"

"I grabbed a bush to help me up and it broke off!" He stared down at his leg in horror. "And I tore my breeches!"

"Never mind them, you're safe. That's all that matters."

"But my leg's bleeding. Look! I think the rock made a hole in my leg!"

She tried to keep calm. "Then we'll bathe it and make it better. Come on, Mousekin, I'll help you back to the cave."

When they had arrived and she had carefully bathed the breeches away from the leg, she tried not to show her concern. The gash was longer and deeper than she had thought possible with such a tumble. She tried to make him smile. "Why, the king would say you were a brave soldier indeed if he saw that, Denis. He'd give you a medal."

But he would not be comforted. "It hurts, Justine. Will it get better?"

"Of course. I'm going to fetch fresh water and bathe it and then I'll tear up my old petticoat to make a bandage." She went swiftly to and from the stream and did what she could to make Denis comfortable.

"But we were going to search for food!"

She patted his hand. "I have a surprise for you. I had some of the corn and fish hidden away in case we couldn't stir from the cave. We'll use that up." She gave him the greater portion and bathed the wound again before they slept. She prayed before they shrine as they did every night and morning, but still she did not sleep herself, feeling she had to be alert to her brother's needs. She dozed off as the first light was breaking the darkness of the cave but was startled awake by a cry from her brother.

"What's the matter?" She came and knelt beside him. "Does it hurt very much?"

"It's a bad pain. I'm trying to be brave, Justine, but it does hurt me so much!"

She undid the makeshift bandage and was horrified by what she saw. The gash was swollen, and all the flesh surrounding it ugly and red. A terrible fear swept over her. She knew what could happen to even simple wounds. People had died of them when they were not properly treated. She kept washing it with water from the stream all day and into the night, almost falling asleep a dozen times in her exhaustion, and still it showed no improvement. There was nothing to eat but a few berries and mushrooms but Denis turned even these aside. During the night a torrid blanket of heat came down and they could hear the far rumble of thunder. It was cool only in the deepest recesses of the cave. As the night wore on Denis became flushed and feverish, crying out with pain. But what could she do? If only Michel were there, he would know what herbs and potions to lay on the wound for healing, but she had no idea what they might be or where she would find them.

At last Denis fell into a troubled sleep and she went out on the ledge, feeling the heat of the night pressing down on her like a smothering wave. Far off over the river the lightning was playing along the hills and thunder rumbled. The howl of a wolf came again, and then another, answering the call. It was the sound of the wilderness—the wilderness that had won after all. They would have to return to the village. She could not sacrifice her brother to her own desire for a life of her own making.

How was she to get Denis back to Tadoussac? Could she carry him? He was sturdily built, and there was the cliff face to climb and a long trail back to the village. If only the trapper would return again, she would take a chance and approach him. But they couldn't wait for that.

Then she remembered the *travois* that the Indians and often the *coureurs de bois* used to transport supplies. It was a kind of sled made of netting supported by two long poles and pulled along the ground. She could make one from branches and the trunks of fallen small trees, and she could use her petticoat or the caribou hide to lay him on. That was the answer. She knelt to give her thanks and then, exhausted with heat and anxiety, she fell asleep.

In the morning Denis was crying with pain, and while she bathed his leg she told him of her plan. His flushed face lit with joy. "We're going home again, then? Really home?"

"Back to the village, Mousekin." Where was home? What awaited her there? She did not dare to consider.

"Then I don't care how much it hurts. I won't cry."

"Then you must be brave, too, while I'm out trying to find poles and sinewy shrubs to make the *travois*. There's no one to hurt you down here. Try to remember silly old King Dagobert while I'm gone."

When she had found the necessary things to make her stretcher, she went back down the path, but even before the mouth of the cave came into view she heard a voice. It was Denis, talking to himself! *Oh, Holy Mother, Blessed Jesus, look after him! He's lost his mind with the fever!* She was about to race down the ledge when she heard movement in the cave. But Denis could not move. It was impossible! She crept as silently as a fox to the cave entrance and peered in. It was Star Boy! He was kneeling beside Denis with a clump of odd-looking plants in his hand. They had slender indented leaves and pretty trumpet-like orange flowers. He was bending over the injured leg and squeezing the plants until a bright orange juice ran from his fingers down over the wound. She had not been quiet enough in her movement, and the Indian boy whirled to see her face framed in the cave opening. With a sudden cry, he swept past her and up the cliff.

Denis sat up. "It feels better, Justine. It feels better! He came as soon as you'd gone and started crumpling up the leaves. The juice makes me feel better. It really does!"

"And I scared him away!" Then she saw the mound of plants on the cave floor. "But look! He's left a lot here. I can go on doing it the way he did." She grabbed a handful of plants and began to work. "Did he speak to you?"

"No, not a word. He looked kind of scared all the while. That's why I was talking to him, to make him feel better. He's my friend, Justine. My leg is going to be all right, isn't it?"

"I know it is, Denis, and we owe that to Star Boy." But where was she to find the right kind of plant when the pile beside her ran out? The answer was there on the ledge when she went out to rest in the shadow of the cliff. Star Boy had left another mound of leaves just where their trail up the cliff face began.

Denis gazed up at her sleepily when darkness came. "I can sleep now, Justine. I'm so very tired."

"Me too, Denis." So tired that even a rock with no boughs on it looked inviting. "We'll both sleep tonight."

"Justine?"

"Go to sleep now, so you'll be better in the morning."

"Yes, but I want to know how he knew what to do."

Justine smiled in the darkness. "The Indians know many things we don't know, Denis. They don't have any medicines brought from France. They make their own from the wild things of the forest. I think Star Boy probably had to gather plants like these for his mother many times to help heal his brothers and sisters or anyone else in the tribe." She felt a sense of peace. "We're lucky we found Star Boy."

She had more reason than ever to think so in the morning. First of all, Denis's wound was so improved that he wanted to get up and walk. "Not for a while," she said. "We'll squeeze more juice all morning and then you can try it in the afternoon."

"But I'm hungry. We have to look for food."

"That can come later. I'll see what I can find alone."

She did not have far to look. As she stepped out into the heat on the ledge, she saw dried roots almost at her feet and a caribou gutskin filled with oil. For winter storage, no doubt—but where had it come from? Star Boy must have found it, but where? "Denis, look here! We can eat! Star Boy has brought us food!"

"What's in the skin?" He leaned on his elbow.

"Probably seal oil. We can use it for lighting the cave as well as for cooking. I'll make a fire and cook the roots and some of the oil together and it will last us all day."

"Where did he get it?"

"I don't know. Let's just give thanks that he's found it and shared it with us. That's all we need to know."

She kept up the treatment all day and when evening came they both sat together on the ledge and watched to see if the boy would come again. But there was no sign of him. The only sounds that broke the silence were the weird, unearthly calls of the loons far below on the river, and the almost human cry of a baby raccoon searching for its mother.

CHAPTER SEVEN

Captured!

In the morning the mystery deepened. Beside the ashes of the fire there was a skin bag made from a caribou leg filled with dried fruit, and a bowl of dried salmon and eel. Justine rejoiced. Wherever he was finding the food, it was evident he intended to look after them. But where *did* he find it? She had to know.

Wherever he went, he must have to go while there was still some light in the sky and in the forest. In the total darkness the wilderness was filled with terrible dangers, even for an Indian boy. As dusk enveloped the vast hills and the burning sun disappeared behind them that evening, she became aware of a small figure hidden behind a clump of shrubs at the end of the ledge. Star Boy! He had come to stay with them, but not too close. She pretended to go in to sleep but crept to the edge of the cave entrance to keep him in sight.

Just before total dark she saw him make a swift move up the cliff trail onto the ridge. She was after him like a rabbit, following silently at a safe distance so that he would not hear her. Two caribou loomed up out of the night, frightening her with their husky forms, and then a bear lumbered across her path on its way to the river to drink. She lost the boy then, but only for a moment. She flitted like a shadow from one tree to another, watching his progress, and then, when the scorched barrier of tree trunks came into view, realized where they were. The burned Montagnais village! He began to scramble up a tree, seeking toeholds in the rough bark. There must be caches of food in the trees! The Montagnais would have stored provisions on racks high in the heavy tree branches. Little wonder she and Denis had not found them when they discovered the abandoned village. She shivered, remembering her reluctance to look up at all. Then she recalled the burned ladder lying amid the debris. It was to reach the cache racks, of course! And there would be stored, safe from wild animals, the remains of last year's harvest of forest and stream, and whatever they had obtained by trade from other tribes or French settlers. Star Boy knew, and they had not guessed.

Watching him, she had a sudden strange feeling of disloyalty towards him. Somehow it was important that he not know she was there. She fled back the way she had come before he could turn and see her. As she lay in the dark breathing thanks to the Blessed Virgin and to Star Boy, she heard a slight movement out on the ledge. He had brought more food, and by this bounty they would all survive.

Denis wakened her to the heat of the next morning. "He's brought some more! Look!"

She looked. There was dried seal meat and a skin bag full of wild rice. The boy was there too, hidden and watching. She pretended not to see him.

Denis saw him as well. "Can't we say thank you?" he whispered.

"Not yet. We might drive him away. We have to let him come to us in his own time."

In the end, though, it was not the boy's growing confidence but a raging storm that brought him to them. It broke just after they had crept to their spruce boughs on the stone slabs to sleep. The rain slashed down in torrents, cascading in waterfalls over the cliff face and between the gigantic hills that made a cavern of the Saguenay's course northward.. Tremendous booms of thunder rebounded off the cliffs and echoed away into the wilderness. Then, when one frighteningly vicious flash of lightning split the sky beyond the cave, she saw the figure creep quietly to a place just inside the entrance and lie down, his body shining with rain. She lay quite still, not daring to move. He had joined them, that was all that mattered.

In the morning he was gone again, but somehow she knew he would return. When he did it was to bring, one at a time, two large pieces of a broken tree. She marvelled at his being able to get them down the trail to the ledge. Then he was gone again and came back with a large bag of dried roots. Carefully he worked at grinding the roots between the two chunks of wood. Then he threw the resulting mash, along with some ashes, into the clay pot over the fire.

Denis was watching him. Justine had warned him not to make a move. "What's he doing that for?"

"He's ground the roots to make us some stew, I think. Now I have to add water and build up the fire. Would you fetch me more dry kindling, Denis?"

Star Boy ran off once more, and again they had complete confidence that he would return. When he did he had his hands full of fresh roots, berries, some unknown green plants, and dried deer meat. He had been back to the Montagnais village, and had also harvested some of the wild things on the forest path.

"Can we eat all those?" Denis eyed the pot warily.

"If Star Boy has gathered them, of course we can." She got the fire burning under the pot with a clear smokeless flame and then watched the Indian boy again as he placed small stones at its heart. When they were hot he scraped them out with a crooked stick and, grabbing them with his hands protected by leaves, dropped them into the pot.

"Why?" Denis whispered.

"They'll cook the stew," Justine told him. "The heat of the stones does that. It's a big stew. It'll do us for many meals."

"But he's only a boy. How does he know how to do all that?"

"He's probably watched his mother and the other women do it a hundred times, Denis. How lucky we are that he has!"

They were so hungry that they could scarcely wait until the stew was done, but before they ate Star Boy made another trip, coming back this time with three broken bark plates. He ate with them, but at some distance on the ledge, keeping his eye not on his food but on them, as if he dared not trust their intentions. The mixture did not taste at all like Maman's delicious rabbit stew, but it was filling and they ate until they were stuffed.

With the storm gone, a new breath of air had blown into the river system, cool and fresh and sweet. They sat out on the ledge looking up at the stars, the Indian boy quiet and at some distance from them.

When night came Star Boy lay down once again inside the cave and watched them as she and Denis knelt together to say their prayers and give thanks. She saw his eyes widen as she drew the ruby red necklace from her shirt and fingered it. Colour and beads were magical to the Indians, she knew that. But she would have to trust that he would not try to steal it from her. It was her own charm against misfortune, her memory of Maman, Papa, and home.

While she lay in the dark, she pictured the boy grinding the roots between the logs, and she remembered with longing her trips to Monsieur Bergeron's mill with Papa to have their own grain ground. She knew it was different up the river, where the *seigneurs* owned and governed large tracts of land reaching down to the St. Lawrence. There the farmers had to take their grain to the *seigneur*'s mill to be ground, and pay for the privilege with a pair of chickens or a sack of grain. In Tadoussac there was no such *seigneur*. The cove and the farms were too small. Monsieur Bergeron was sometimes paid with a special animal skin from the fort or a side of pork. It had been at Monsieur Bergeron's watermill that she had first made friends with Gervaise. Even though they had come together from France, it was only at the mill that they had begun to talk together and confide their hopes and dreams. But how far away he seemed now. Would she ever see him again? What had happened to make him break fath with them? If only he had come as he had promised, everything would be different now, and so many things possible.

The week went by filled with a strange kind of peace. The heat came again and each day melted into the next. She lost count of the days and knew only that they seemed to be wrapped in safety since Star Boy had come. While Denis's leg was healing it was the Indian boy who fetched water from the stream and the wild plants and berries that were their food. One day he brought back a rabbit, freshly killed.

"Where did he get it?" Denis wanted to know.

"He's made a snare, I think, and caught it that way. The meat will be good for all of us."

"Like Maman's rabbit pie?"

"Even better!" She smiled at him, not wanting him to brood about the past. "We'll cook it in the pot with all the wild plants and roots he's brought us."

"Will he ever talk to us?"

"I don't know. Be patient. He has to trust us in every way before we try to teach him our language."

It was his own language he used one morning as he stood at the foot of the trail up the cliff, pointing and exclaiming in a burst of strange words.

"He's speaking!" Denis eyed him with astonishment. "What does he want?"

"I think he wants us to follow him. Is your leg strong enough?"

"Oh, yes. It doesn't hurt any more at all."

They followed him up the path and into the forest, winding among the huge trees on a trail of his own. He stopped to pull lumps of resinous pitch from the wounded bark of a balsam tree and gave it to them to chew. It was delicious! Then he went on to the grey hole of a beech tree and scrambled up it to find a squirrel's secret. He reached a wiry arm down into a hole in the tree trunk and drew his hand out filled with beech nuts.

"More food, Denis! Nuts the squirrels hid last year! Come on, stuff your pockets and your shirt with them. They're good to eat."

When they were finished they had gathered milkweed pods, wild onion, grapes, and many other good things for the cave storehouse. It was while Star Boy was tearing up spruce bark as they sat and watched from the forest floor that they heard a sudden noise. A huge rumbling filled the air around them. The ground beneath them trembled. Star Boy grabbed them both and pulled them far back into a grove of thickly intertwined pine.

"What is it?" Denis asked. "Everything's shaking!"

The answer came in a moment as a herd of caribou thundered by, their hoofs sending pine needles and forest debris flying. She supposed they might have been frightened by a pack of wolves high in the hills.

Star Boy released Justine and Denis and went on with his work at the spruce bark.

"How did he know what was coming?" Denis wanted to know.

"I think he knows everything about the forest, Denis, and we know almost nothing. I've no idea what he's making now, but I can see he's done it before."

At last they saw what it was, a net fashioned from strips of bark bound together with sinewy lengths from the tree trunk. "Now see what he can do," Justine rejoiced. "And we couldn't make one at all!"

Star Boy set off at once with them at his heels. Always they moved with great caution because the forest was filled with danger. When they came to water they discovered he had led them to a small waterfall with a deep pool at its base. They watched as he quickly gathered some wildflowers and leaves and knelt at the fall, speaking softly in his own tongue.

Denis whispered, "It's like the shrine we made in the cave."

"It's to the Great Spirit, Denis. They see Him everywhere," Justine said softly.

Denis lifted a puzzled face to hers. "But isn't He ours, too?"

Justine cast him a startled glance and then pulled him hastily to his knees beside her. It was right to give thanks with Star Boy for all the good that had come to them with him.

A great blue heron rose with a rush of huge wings from the shady reaches of the pond as Star Boy himself rose to cast the net into the still, dark waters. In a moment the pond was alive with fish, leaping and gleaming in the sunlight. Justine laughed for joy. "Denis, we'll never go hungry as long as Star Boy is with us. The Blessed Virgin has sent him. We must say special prayers tonight."

When they knelt at the cave shrine later they tried to urge Star Boy to join them. But he remained sitting where he always sat, cross-legged near the mouth of the cave, watching them with wide, solemn eyes.

During the evenings, when the food was gathered and they relaxed on the ledge gazing at the river far below, they taught him the pebble game. When he won and laughed aloud with delight, Denis said, "He must have played that before! Why don't we try to teach him our words?"

"We'll try," Justine agreed. "You draw pictures on the cave floor with a stick and I'll say the words that go with them over and over."

But Star Boy laughingly grabbed the stick and drew his own pictures, one of a bear and another of a huge bird they did not recognize. He pointed to the latter and said one word over and over, as they had done, but try as they would, they could not get their tongues around it. "Anyway, he draws better than I do," Denis admitted. "The big bird looks as if it's going to fly away."

"It looks alive, like the cave drawing," Justine said. She longed for the words to communicate. It made her realize how lucky she and Denis were to be able to read and write. Few in their village could. But Papa had been the town scribe in France, and Maman convent-educated, so they were able to help others. As chief clerk of the fur fort Papa had been important, just as he had been at home in France, writing letters and preparing important documents for the villagers who did not have his skill, in exchange for a basket of grain or some salt bacon. She had never realized how important words were until she could find none to reach out with to Star Boy.

She knew how he would learn. If they were ever able to return home to the village, he would learn there. He would hear the words and join in the life of the settlement just as they did, and then the language would become a part of him. But would they ever go back? She lay thinking about it the night after Star Boy had shown his skill at drawing, while the two boys were curled up asleep. Even though she had told Denis there was no settlement up the river, how did she know for sure? There might be a small one they could make for, perhaps beyond the cape called Eternity, where settlers might help them go up the St. Lawrence River to Quebec and the convent. She recalled that when French strangers arrived in Tadoussac, they were always welcomed with hospitality. Surely other settlements would take in children who had lost their home, even an Indian boy, especially a Montagnais. What she had to do was to go up the Saguenay to find the point of land from which she could see farther into the unknown. She knew there was a point of land somewhere up there because Michel and his friends had said they had camped on one when they went hunting, a sandy spit that gave haven for a canoe or two, and a place to light a fire. Suddenly she was determined. She would go in the morning, following a trail along the cliff edge in order to find a way down to the river. It was worth the danger because now Star Boy was here to look after Denis.

At the fire the next morning she told Denis of her plan. He objected with a flood of tears. "I don't want to be left here alone!"

"But you're not alone, that's why I'm going. Star Boy will look after you and keep you safe."

"But why can't I go with you?"

"Because I can travel more swiftly alone. I want to see if there's a settlement we can head for up the river anywhere, or perhaps one of our own brigades, like Pierre Clermont's, coming home."

"But why can't we all stay here? We're getting enough to eat now—and I like living in the cave."

"There are other things to think of." She did not mention the coming of winter, when there would be no food, when the snow would lie thick on all the hills and even some of the Indians would starve to death. "Trust me. I'm doing this for all of us. If we find a settlement, Star Boy can come with us."

"You'll come back soon, won't you?" Denis clung to her arm.

"Of course, very soon." She tried to show Star Boy by mime that she was going and leaving Denis in his care. Then she went on her way up to the trail.

The forest was eerily silent in the heat of the morning, with only the sounds of small animals scuttering across her path and the shrill piping of some demanding bird in the treetops. When she had been following the cliff edge for half an hour she decided to change her plan. "If I go down to the river shore, I'll find the sand-bar more easily," she thought. "I can't see it from up here because of overhanging rock."

The way down was not easy. She tore her hands and jerkin on the sharp projecting rocks and yet she was thankful for them; they were her toeholds on her descent to the river. She reached the bottom at last and the wide waters of the Saguenay lay at her feet. What a river it was! With a high wind blowing down here in the cavern between the hills, it had waves like the ocean. She crept along the shore from tree to tree, hiding in case there should be an enemy here or on the opposite shore, but she was quite unprepared for the sound of voices and burst of laughter that echoed with startling suddenness in front of her. By the time she looked through the trees and saw the sandy spit she was seeking, it was too late. A man was watching her from a clump of spruce.

What had she blundered into? A hasty camp made by some *coureurs de bois*, probably because of the wind and high water. They were strangers; she had never seen them before. As she tried to run, a hand grasped her shoulder.

"Hey! Look here! Look what I've found! A runaway!"

"A runaway! So you want to be a *coureur*, do you, big fellow?"

"He's come to the right place, eh, Gaspard? We can put him to work."

"He can be our potboy at the campfire. What do you think, Jean-Luc? Is there room for one more in our brigade?"

"Eh, why not, Jacques? This one will give us a little entertainment, no doubt!"

The last one to speak frightened her the most. He was a big, evil-looking man, his clothes torn and dirty, his beard and hair in disarray, and his face pockmarked with old diseases. He seized her tightly by the arm and held her face close to his own. "Now, what's your name, boy?"

"Justin, *monsieur*. My name is Justin." She tried to appear unafraid, deeply thankful in her heart that she was in boy's clothing.

"Justin, eh? See, my friends? No family name! He doesn't want us to know where he comes from."

"But we know where he's going, Jean-Luc! In the morning, when the wind has gone, he's coming with us into fur country."

"We'll be off before dawn," Jacques called out. "We'll see what you're made of, lad."

"You can make yourself useful right away," Jean-Luc ordered. "Gather us some firewood. No big pieces,

mind. Just the kind to set the fire going for a quick meal."
He gave her an evil grin. "If you behave yourself you
might have a sup or two yourself. I'll wager you've
had to collect firewood at home," and he winked at her,
"wherever that is." She nodded dumbly, afraid to speak
too much for fear of betraying herself as a girl. She went
about the business of gathering the wood, keeping her
distance from the company of men on the riverbank.

There were three canoes drawn up on the spit, two
with sails that sped their passage across lakes and were
used as tents at night. Justine guessed that the *coureurs*
were starting out on their last venture into the wilderness
before winter set in. She watched them secretly as she
picked up the wood and placed it near the campfire. They
were the roughest-looking men she had ever seen, coarse
in appearance and language, their speech laced with
swearing. There was no telling what danger lay in wait
for her if she did not make her escape, and soon. The
fact that they had accepted her as a boy could not last.
What would happen when they discovered the truth?

She tried to appear at ease beside the campfire as
they ate. They feasted on fresh fish, roast venison, and
peas, but she knew their fare would get simpler as they
rode farther into the wilderness. They would likely
eat little other than *sagamité*, soup made from a little
ground maize and whatever else they could find to pitch
in. As they began to tell stories and crude jokes after
eating, Jean-Luc dragged her from the edge of the forest,
keeping his face and body close to her own. She laughed
with them; it would never do to appear different. But she
breathed more freely when, one by one, stupefied by the
liquor they had drunk and exhausted by the long day's
journey from some far place, they fell asleep. When their
snores filled the night, she looked from one to another
to make sure they were in no state to stop her, and crept
away to the canoes. Asking forgiveness of the Blessed

Virgin, she rifled the food store under one of them and found a huge hunk of bread and some salt pork and stuffed both in her shirt. Then she began to climb.

In the dark the way was almost impossible. At one point there was nowhere for her foot to go. *Here's where I shall be in the morning when they wake, and they'll come after me!* And then she looked up and there was a young birch tree growing out of a rock. She grasped it and pulled herself up. As she did so, a bird's nest fell out of it, dropping far below to the river. She moved slowly and carefully, aware that she could fall there too. When she reached the top she could go no farther. She was worn out with the climb and the events of the day. And in the night, even more than in the day, the unknown lurked on every trail. She would have to find a thicket of trees to hide in, but where? Her eyes were accustomed to the darkness by now and she crept along, wishing for a moon to light her way but catching only now and then a glimpse of the stars through the branches. Suddenly she was enveloped by a cloud of mosquitoes. They were in her eyes, her nose, her mouth, caught in her hair. Then she saw a hole at the base of a massive pine. A fox's den! What a wonderful hiding-place from mosquitoes and men—if she could scare the fox away! But the hole was empty, abandoned by its owner for one better, perhaps. She shut her mind to the smell as she crawled in. There could be fleas in here, too, but when she reached a stream she could rid herself of those. What were a few fleas to the dangers she faced with the strangers?

Once inside she was too exhausted to think of fleas or the discomfort of the root floor. She was asleep at once.

When she woke the darkness was still there but a ribbon of light was showing beyond the den entrance. *Where was she? What had happened?* Then she smelled the rank odour of fox and she knew. Quickly she scrambled out and found the trail to the cliff. The men would be gone by now and she must be safe. But it was not so. They were breaking camp with the first light of dawn, and the big fellow, Jean-Luc, was shouting at his fellows and pointing up the cliff. *He was coming up after her! He had no intention of letting her get away! She must fly!*

Heedless of her direction, she began to run. Only when full daylight came did she stop, breathless, and fling herself down in a carpet of deep fern. She was trembling from head to foot with fear and exhaustion. But no one had followed her, she was sure of that. They would be on their way now, the rough ones, paddling their canoes and singing their songs, and shouting their oaths at one another. Soon the wilderness would swallow them for a few months and she need never see them again. She leaned against a tree trunk and chewed ravenously at the bread and pork. She had been given little to eat at the campfire the night before, and she needed strength to go on. And go on she did, after she had relished the last crumb, trying to find a trail she could identify. When the sun had reached its noon height she was still lost—and hungry again. There was a lightening of the dark forest ahead of her and she made her way carefully towards it, aware that it might mean an Indian encampment. She found instead a great area of forest destroyed by fire, perhaps set ablaze by a single flash of lightning. The clearing was covered with the pinkish blue blossoms of fireweed, but there was another kind of plant growing around the charred stumps and blackened trunks of the survivors. Blueberries! She could eat! There were masses of them, many unripe, but some ready for picking. Her hands and mouth were stained with them when she had had her fill.

It was time to find her way back to the river. The *coureurs* would be long gone and she must find the river trail to reach the safety of the cave again. She had little thought of Denis and Star Boy; she expected them to be safe. It was her own need to get back to them that mattered.

In another hour she knew she was lost. She came again on the burned clearing. She had travelled in a complete circle. What could she do?

By nightfall she still had not found the river. She had avoided returning to the burned area yet again by dint of making frequent gashes with her knife in the trees so that she would not cover the same ground twice. She felt the direction of the wind and tried to follow that because more often than not it blew down the river from the north. It was growing dusk when she realized in astonishment that she had made her way back to the very place where she had sought shelter the night before. And there was the fox's den! Praise God! It could be her shelter for the night again, and the river could not be far away. She checked first to make sure it was still empty and then crawled in, grateful for the dark recess that protected her.

She was scarcely inside when she heard a whistle—long and low, like some wandering night-bird's. But *was* it a bird? She listened, trying to still the thumping of her heart. Could it be Indians? She had heard that they signalled to one another by whistling. She lay trembling, trying to be brave. But sleep overcame her and it was morning when she woke, almost suffocated by the stench of fox and the smallness of her hiding-place. She peered out and saw a young deer pick its delicate way through the forest. Would it be going in search of water? She needed some desperately. Her mouth was swollen with thirst. She followed the animal at a safe distance, trying to keep downwind from it so that it would not smell her and bound away. They came at last to a forest stream with a white froth of rapids where she waded in, bathed her face, and drank deeply from water cupped in her hands. The deer had gone, leaping for safety when it saw her. She was as ill at ease as the deer, feeling as if every tree had eyes. She found a clump of shrubs to hide in until she knew the way was safe. But the whistle came again. It could not have been a night-bird then. It *must* be Indians! What could she do? There was nowhere safe to hide. She tried to reassure herself that most Indians were good to children, even taking in orphans of other tribes as their own. Then she remembered how Denis had found Star Boy, and felt reassured no more.

She moved along the clifftop trying to find the trail, stealing like a shadow from tree to tree. When the whistle came a third time she threw herself to the ground in terror. Whoever they were, they were almost as close as her own breath. She tried to be brave, placing herself with a prayer in the care of the Blessed Virgin. Then she waited for the loud savage shout, the feel of a vengeful hand on her body, or the piercing pain of an arrow. None came. She raised her head slowly. He was standing by the tree, gazing at her, his eyes bright with expectation. *Star Boy! He had come in search of her and found her!*

In a great surge of relief, she broke into tears and, sobbing, ran forward to fling herself on him in gratitude. But suddenly he seemed taller, older than he was, smiling but regarding her with a kind of fierce pride and independence that made her hesitate. Then the moment was gone and, pointing into the forest, he beckoned her to follow him.

He travelled swiftly and silently and she was on his heels. She was the leader no longer, if she ever had been. The wisdom of the wilderness had brought him to her. He had been taught to follow a trail by a scratch on tree bark, a single trodden leaf, a broken twig, and he had found her. It was Star Boy's wisdom and his alone that would keep them safe in their hidden encampment and help them survive.

CHAPTER EIGHT

A Rainbow in the Night

"Where have you been? Where have you been, Justine?" Denis was waiting for them at the foot of the cliff trail on the ledge. He flung himself at her, sobbing.

She folded him in her arms. "There now, Mousekin. Don't carry on so. I'm back safe now."

"I thought you'd never come back again. I thought you were dead! Where did you go?"

"It's too much to tell now. Star Boy saved me. What have you been doing while I've been gone? Did you eat?"

"Yes, he brought food every day and cooked it for us both. Then he tried to tell me what he was going to do. He kept pointing up the cliff and talking. But I didn't know what he meant. Then he went away and didn't come back and I thought I was going to die!"

"But you didn't and we must give thanks that we're all back together again." She beckoned to Star Boy to join them at the shrine, and to her joy he came slowly and knelt beside them. She poured her heart out in gratitude, drawing the two boys close to her with her arms around their shoulders. This time Star Boy did not pull away but gazed at her intently with a puzzled, questioning look on his face.

Prayers said, she looked around the cave. There was some disorder, bits of bark flung here and there, fish bones scattered on the cave floor, but from a rock projection near the back of the cave hung the skinned carcasses of two small animals. How had he managed that without her knife?

Denis had the answer. "It's a squirrel and a porcupine and we went to the village and found a scraper." He pointed to a sharp bone tool lying on the rock. "That's how he took the skins off. He took some of it off with our turtle shell. I helped him."

"Then we can feast tonight. It will be like a coming-home party, a *veillée* in the village for the *coureurs de bois*. I'll cook it all myself and show how grateful I am to Star Boy." She gave Denis another swift hug. "And to you, Denis, for being brave."

But her resolve was not enough to keep her awake after the long hours of fear and flight. When she lay down in the shelter of the cave she fell asleep at once. She woke to find the sun far down the sky and the whole cave fragrant with the smell of cooking meat. Star Boy and Denis had prepared the feast and they all ate hungrily.

Later, before the sun had set, Star Boy disappeared. When he came back down the path he carried a short hollow log and a sturdy piece of limb like a club. He set the log on the rock in the cave and began to beat it in a steady rhythm. Then he picked up the log in one hand and beat it with the club in the other and began to dance round and round the cave. They mimicked him, treading the shale floor in a circle, faster and faster, their own excitement growing, until he seemed to reach the height of his drumming and stopped as suddenly as he had begun. They fell to the floor exhausted. She knew it had been a dance of joy to welcome her home, just as the villagers welcomed the ships from France with dancing and prayers. Star Boy was rejoicing that they were all together again.

In their celebration, though, they had forgotten the need for silence. She remembered it suddenly, alert for any sound overhead. But none came.

When the boys lay sleeping, she went to the fire to reassure herself that it was not smoking, and then she sat relishing the cool sweet air that flowed up from the river valley after the intense heat of the day. Her thoughts flickered like the last pale flames of the fire. *We're becoming like Indians now, eating Indian food, dancing Indian dances, learning to live in the wilderness. Where will it all end?* But it was not for her to know the end. They were alive and together again, that was the miracle. Star Boy too. Star Boy was one of them, truly one of them, and she would never let him go from them. Just as he watched over her, she would watch over him, and one day, when rescue came, he would go upriver with them to another settlement. She took one last look at the stars and went in to sleep.

A week later Star Boy had caught no more meat in his snares. They had exhausted the supply of dried fish, meat, and corn from the burned village, and they had to live on roots, green plants, and berries. But they were still hungry. Denis complained of feeling empty when he went to sleep.

They managed to catch a few more fish where the stream had been teeming with them some weeks before, but it was not enough. Justine wondered if the heat that had held the forest and canyon in thrall for weeks on end, with only a few days of respite, had sent the fish scurrying for shelter in some deep pond farther downstream where she and the boys dared not venture, and the animals to the cool of their lairs.

They were out one early morning, foraging as always for their daily food, when Denis, parting the bushes to look down at the river, called out softly, "There's something down there!"

Canoes! Perhaps it was another brigade! Justine raced to his side but saw nothing.

"No, not down there, across the river on the other side. Look! There are two of them!"

"Moose! A mother and her calf! They're trying to cross the river!"

"But they can't!" Denis grabbed her arm as if she could do something about it. "It's too rough there. There are rocks!"

Star Boy was at their side in an instant, watching with them. Justine wanted to cry out, "Go back! Go back!" Perhaps if the baby moose had heard a shout it might have retreated in fear. But she could not even cry out to it. She was high on the precipice and it was down in the river, far down.

Suddenly a huge wave blown high by the wind that swept down the Saguenay bore down on the calf. Its mother was swimming strongly against the current and making for the shore, but the calf was too weak. It went down under the wave, surfaced and struggled, went down again, and then, limp and motionless, floated to the surface of the water. A sudden gust of wind bearing around the bend in the river swept the calf's body against the rocks on their side, and there it lodged. The cow moose bawled her anguish from the bank. With a triumphant shout, Star Boy snatched the knife from Justine's belt and slipped and slithered down the cliff, taking the path she herself had taken when she had come upon the *coureurs de bois*. The cow fled in panic into the trees on the shore.

"What's he doing?" Denis stared after Star Boy in astonishment.

"It's meat! Don't you see, Denis, it's meat for us to eat!"

"The calf? But we can't eat it!"

"Of course we can! The little thing's not alive any more. We can't help it, but it can help us! If we cure the meat we'll have food for months. Come on, we have work to do." She hurried back to the cave and gathered up the caribou hide. With Denis following, she scrambled down to the shore. They stopped when they came upon Star Boy kneeling beside the drowned calf, his hands on the still form.

"What's he saying?" Denis whispered.

"I don't know. Perhaps he's thanking the calf for coming to us and saying a blessing just as we say blessings."

But the blessing was over in a moment, and with strong thrusts of the knife Star Boy slashed at the animal and began to dismember it.

Denis turned away, his face white and strained, but Justine hardened herself against the sight of so much blood. This was food that would keep them alive.

Some time later they made a carry-all of the caribou hide and filled it with meat. Together they carried it up the cliff face and back to the cave. Star Boy was grinning from ear to ear and talking endlessly in his own language, and Justine and Denis were shouting with glee at the feast to come. And feast they did, savouring the strong taste of the meat and its coarse texture.

Sleepy with food, having seen no need to scrimp on helpings, they built a drying rack on which to lay the rest of the meat to cure it. For that they needed a smoky fire, and they set it closer to the entrance to the cave so the smoke did not betray them by rising into the forest.

They would not be hungry for a long time to come. The calf had done well for them.

While they tended the fire they played the pebble game again, throwing the stones to the ground like dice to see how many of one colour turned up for the players. Star Boy made a variation on this game. He brought the broken wooden bowl from the cave, set the stones with colours dark and light in the centre, then thumped the bowl to make them jump. The one who had the most light or dark sides up was the winner.

Denis was lucky; he won four times in a row. He and Justine were startled then when Star Boy grabbed the bowl and swept the stones to the ledge with an impatient hand. Denis frowned up at Justine. "Why did he do that?"

"Because he wanted to win, silly goose. We all want to win, even you."

"I'd never do anything like that."

"Oh yes you would, and you have. Remember when Henri Bergeron's young brother Marcel beat you in the foot race at the May Day Festival? You sat down and cried and kicked your heels on the ground."

Denis looked at her with an innocent air. "Did I do that?"

"Yes you did, and you'll do it again, perhaps, if you get disappointed and angry." She began to gather up the coloured pebbles, but suddenly, his face split with a wide grin, Star Boy was ahead of her, offering her the bowl and swooping down on the ledge to retrieve every stone. In a moment they were all laughing together again.

Then, unexpectedly, Denis said sadly, "I wish we could go home and play our own games."

"We shall, one day." But there was little assurance in her voice. She seldom thought of rescue now, only of survival. "Then you'll become a fine *seigneur* and own a great tract of land up the river. I'll live with you and wear velvet and lace. Perhaps I'll play the spinet and dance the minuet, just the way the *seigneur*'s daughters do now."

Denis said, "They don't all do that, Papa told me even the *seigneurs* have to work on the land with their helpers sometimes, and all the family, too, just as we used to."

Justine laughed ruefully. "Maybe, but I think they'd be dressed a little better than I am right now!" She looked down at her ragged boy's clothes. She had tried to keep them clean by washing them and Denis's piece by piece in the stream and drying them on the cliff ledge, but there were rips and tears she could not mend without needle and thread. At least they had no worry about footgear. For the most part they ran about with bare feet like Star Boy.

She often wondered how he saw her. He surely must know by now that she was a girl, even though she bathed alone at the stream each morning while the boys were still in the cave. But what did it matter? They were living as close and warm as a family could be and, were it not for winter coming on, they could go on indefinitely.

Denis was helping Star Boy to pile more branches on the fire. "I know what I want when I'm a grand *seigneur*. A horse! Shall I have one, do you think?"

"Of course. Maybe two! I remember when the first horse came to the colony from the old country."

"When was that?"

"Three years ago. It was going to Quebec as a gift to the governor from the Community of Habitants, the company Papa worked for. The ship that brought it put into Tadoussac and you should have seen the happy faces! You'd think the King of France himself was coming ashore, instead of a humble horse!"

"Perhaps the farmers were thinking of the horses they'd left at home in France." Denis looked at her longingly. "I'd have a happy face if I had a horse."

I would, too, she thought, *especially now. We could all ride away to find another settlement far from Louis Gaudin.* "Go to sleep now and dream of horses," she advised, "and maybe your dream will come true."

Not an hour had passed when, lying awake in the dark, Justine saw Star Boy creeping out of the cave. Her heart lurched with fear. Was he going to leave them? Was he going to try to find his own people, wherever they had fled?

Denis was still awake. "What's he doing?"

"I don't know. Wait here and I'll see." Aware of a strange brightness, she crept to the mouth of the cave and peered out

Star Boy was standing in a gap between the shrubs on the ledge, staring up at the sky. He was as still as the rock on which he stood. Then suddenly he fell to his knees, his head to the rock ledge.

She knew why at once. The whole northern sky above the forest wilderness was alight with colour. Streamers of yellow and green, blue and violet and red hung from the heavens, flowing and wavering in the surrounding darkness like magical veils flung by an invisible hand. The light was reflected in the river below and charged the air all around them as if they were imprisoned inside a precious jewel.

Denis had crept to her side. "What is it?" he whispered. "Is the world coming to an end?"

Justine put her arm around him. "Not yet, Denis. It's what Papa used to call the rainbow of the night. Don't you remember watching it from the cabin door?" She tightened her arm about his shoulders. "There's nothing to be afraid of. We don't know why it comes but we've seen it before." And always before the cold of winter set in, she remembered. Always. She tried to suppress a shiver. How foolish she had been not to mark the passage of days on a tree limb with her knife. It was too late for that now. The days slid into one another, all alike in heat and sun and wind.

Star Boy raised his head slowly and looked at them. His eyes were big with fear and wonder mixed. Justine smiled at him reassuringly and his whole body seemed to relax. "He won't be scared if we're not," she said. "Smile at him, Denis!"

They watched while the streamers came and went, flickering and dancing down the sky. Then gradually the rainbow colours faded and they were left looking up at the stars. "Indians can tell the time of year by the stars," Justine said. "I wish Star Boy could tell us if summer's nearly over."

"Can't we try to teach him some words again?" Denis asked. "He could tell us then."

"We can try again. Tomorrow we'll find some birch-bark and write on it with some charred clay or burnt wood from the fire."

The following day the teaching seemed to go better than it had the first time. Star Boy sat out on the ledge with his eyes on the northern sky most of the morning, as if waiting for another magical spectacle, but in the afternoon he joined in the lessons and somehow got his tongue around the strange words. They all laughed together and Justine wished she knew whether he really understood or if it was just another game to him. They had tried more than once to mimic his words, without success.

It was Star Boy who began the next game. He brought two curved sticks from the forest and a round stone from the cliff edge and batted the stone at them, waiting for whoever had the other stick to bat it back. They were so boisterous in their playing that Justine had to remind them to keep their voices down. Somehow they had lived in safety for so long that they had forgotten to be careful. It seemed that the forest and all things in it belonged to them. Apart from the odd trapper going on his silent way to inspect his traps, there had been no one. She was thankful that at least the Iroquois had not returned. She feared them the most. And she knew that if they did return, the three of them would have no defence against them.

CHAPTER NINE

Tunnel to Safety

It was the Iroquois she thought of first when she heard the voices the following day. The morning had begun with a heavy mist hanging on rock and bough. The heat was still there, made more intense by the blanket of fog that surrounded them.

Star Boy, with his unerring sense of direction, led the way to the stream through the frightening darkness, to fetch water. He caught a turtle at the water's edge and held it up triumphantly. It would make a fine change from moose meat. Then, hands and exposed parts of their bodies bathed in the cold water, they stole back to the heat of the ledge and the dark recesses of the cave.

It was too hot to light the fire and they ate the cold remnants of the previous day's cooking, washing the meal down with clear water from the stream. While they were lying about, making an effort to be interested in drawing pictures and making words, the voices came. At first they thought they had heard an echo coming up from the river, but then Justine realized the sounds were directly over their heads. Close! Too close!

The Iroquois, she thought at once. *The Iroquois have come back to search for more spoils in the Montagnais village, or to pillage another, perhaps even Tadoussac!*

Denis huddled close to her. "I heard somebody say 'lost'."

"You heard that?"

"Yes, I swear I did!"

"Then it must be some of our own people! Not the Iroquois at all."

Star Boy was standing stock-still inside the cave, every nerve alert.

They listened again, scarcely daring to breathe. There was an explosion of voices as if in deep quarrelling. Then she made out some words, although, with the sounds muffled by the rock above, it was hard at first to recognize the speakers.

"How does he expect us to find them after all this time?"

Another voice, more strident than the first, answered. "They've been gone for weeks and weeks! If we find the heap of bones the animals have left we'll be lucky."

"Aye, and he wouldn't want those dropped on his doorstep," growled a third voice.

"Yes, but he won't pay us unless we take back some proof we've searched and found nothing."

"He promised me enough to outfit me for a trip into the wilderness next spring. There's no other way I'll get the supplies."

Justine felt herself grow rigid. Now she knew who "he" was. Louis Gaudin! He had promised some young men of the village money and supplies if they came in search of her and brought her back to him. It shouldn't be too hard to guess who the searchers were. There were few families in the settlement, almost always outnumbered by the fur traders and the Montagnais Indians who lived in a huddle of crudely built cabins near the chapel, and even they went home to the wilderness when the hunting season began.

The voices came again. "I wish we'd never started. Now what do we do?"

"Search every nook and cranny, I suppose. Maybe there'll be some clothes dropped in haste, so we have something to take back to him. He's a fool to go on hoping at this point."

"We'll have to fan out and try to find our way in this fog."

"Yes, but we daren't get too far from the cliff—or too close. Either way we're lost, in the forest or in the river, and rewards won't do us much good in either place!"

"Fan out it is then. You take the trail northwards, I'll take it south, and Philippe can search around here until we get back. But take care!"

In the depths of the cave they all exchanged startled gazes. Star Boy went to stand guard at the entrance. Denis set down the bowl he was carrying. They both looked to Justine. She had heard every word and she knew what was to come. If rewards had been promised, the searchers would leave no trail unexplored. So many of the young men were eager to try their hand in the fur trade and experience the dangers of life in the wilderness. They longed for the freedom from farm duty away from their families, and for the excitement of new adventures. All they needed was the means of escape. The chance to get a reward of either supplies or money was too much for them to resist. Justine knew it was only a matter of time before they discovered the hiding-place.

She felt a sudden hopelessness. Had she and Denis and Star Boy come through so much only to have it end like this, being taken captive back to the village and the life she dreaded? Was Louis Gaudin to be her master after all? She was so tangled in despair and confusion that she scarcely heard Denis speaking.

"I know where we can hide."

She turned to him, her mind groping for answers. "Did you say something?"

"Yes, I said I know where we can hide."

"How can we hide?" She spoke almost bitterly. "If we go up on the cliff the one left behind will see us. And then it'll be all up with us. They'll drag us back to the village."

Star Boy's eyes darted from one to the other as they spoke. Denis asked, "Would it be so bad—going back, I mean? Shall we have to live in a cave for ever?"

For a moment she was silent. She knew they could not live in the cave for ever. She had hoped that long before this they would have seen a friendly brigade, one of those they could trust, coming down the river. She would have flagged it down and told the travellers everything, sure that a real friend would take them up the St. Lawrence to a convent or at least protect them when they returned to the village. But now she was defenceless. And there were others involved, Denis and Star Boy. If they all returned to the village there would be a life for the boys, at least. But her whole being rebelled against returning. If the plans the village gossips had for her were fulfilled, she would be Louis Gaudin's handmaiden and then his wife and all the joy would be gone from her life. There was an alternative: she could run away into the forest alone and leave the boys to be discovered. But what means would the searchers use to get information from them about the trail she had taken? How could she trust them when she knew their motive was money for a trip to the wilderness?

Denis had spoken again, almost in a whisper. "I said I know where we can hide."

"But there's no place to go! We can't go up on the ridge. They'd see us!"

"Oh, it isn't up on the ridge. It's right here where we are."

"Denis, how can there be anywhere here? We can't crawl under a slab of rock!"

"But we can crawl into a hole."

"What hole?"

"Behind our little shrine. Perhaps the Blessed Virgin showed it to me."

"I've never seen a hole there. How did you see it?"

"When we were praying I opened my eyes. Just a little bit, Justine," he hastened to add. "Just a tiny bit! And I saw a mouse run into the crack behind that stone slab."

"A mouse! We can't go where a mouse goes!"

"Oh, it's bigger than that." Denis moved behind the shrine and pulled down the flat table of stone that leaned against the end cave wall. "See what I mean?"

"There is a hole! But it's not big enough for the three of us to crawl inside. That's no answer!"

"But it is! It gets bigger when you go in!"

Justine looked at him in astonishment. "How do you know?"

"Because I went in there and hid when you and Star Boy went away and I thought you weren't coming back." Denis seemed almost frightened at his confession. "I thought I'd be safe if the Iroquois came back."

"But why didn't you tell me you'd found a hole?"

"I thought you'd scold me for going in without asking you first." Denis looked at her hopefully. "You told me I wasn't ever to go anywhere without asking you first."

"This could be the answer, but we'll have to move quickly. When the searchers come together again, I'm sure they'll look among the bushes on the face of the cliff." She turned to Star Boy, who had not moved all the time they had been speaking. She motioned that she was going to crawl into the hole. But he kept his distance, a look of alarm on his face. Then she remembered Michel telling her how, even in the fort, the Indians avoided the dark confined spaces. With encouraging words and gestures she finally got him to kneel by the entrance, Denis across from him, as she began to worm her way into the narrow passage on all fours. Suddenly she knew the truth of Denis's statement. The passage widened and there was a spacious area, certainly big enough for the three of them to take shelter in. To her surprise, the air was not stale deep within the rock. From somewhere a fresh breeze was blowing and she could hear the sound of water. Then she saw another passage leading off the first, dimly lit by some strange light. She bent double again and made her way along it, her clothes wet with condensation from the walls that hemmed her in.

When she came on the cave-room, it was like a miracle. It reminded her of the chapel at home in the village when the morning sun came in at the windows. Here the sun came in too; it burned its way through the morning mist and filtered through what appeared to be long fissures above her head. It shone with a kind of unearthly gleam on a large pond at her feet. Then she saw where the water came from—a narrow ribbon of waterfall, probably from a spring, bubbling down one wall of the cave. She knew where it went. It flowed underground from the pond at her feet and down the cliff beyond their own hiding-place to the Saguenay. There were dozens of such ribbons of fresh water streaming down the hills, and she had found the source of one.

She had also found, thanks to Denis, a place where they could hide in safety. But there was no time to lose. She knelt on the stone floor again and squirmed back to the waiting boys in the outer cave.

There was no way she could explain what she had in mind to Star Boy. But she could to Denis. "You heard what they said. They would be happy if they could find some trace of us to take back. Well, we'll leave a trace and more."

"What can we leave?" Denis gaped at her in bewilderment.

"My girl's clothing—some of it, anyway." She hauled the bundle out from the rock shelf. "They can have no notion that I'm dressed in Gervaise's brother's clothes." The mere mention of his name stabbed her with unbearable disappointment. How could he have let them down so? If it had been otherwise she and Denis might now be safe in a convent in Quebec with the Ursulines. *But then what of Star Boy? What would have happened to him?* She shook off her uncertainties.

"What about me? Shall I leave anything?"

"Yes, your leather jerkin. You haven't needed it anyway, in the heat." And she hoped with all her heart that they would not still be there when he needed it again.

"Is that enough?"

"I think so. They'll know we've been here. Come now, we have to hurry and leave the cave as if it had been deserted for a long time."

As soon as she began to hide plates and bowls and implements under rocks and in crevices, Star Boy saw what she was about and came to help her. When all was safely stowed away, they scattered a few bones on the cave floor, and grabbed some food to carry with them inside their shirts. They left the fire to Star Boy. When he was finished no one could have told there had been a cooking site there. The cave had an air of desertion, of some disorder, too, as if there had been a struggle.

Quickly she signalled the two boys to go before her into the narrow passage. Hesitating only a moment, with fear on his face, Star Boy went first, with Denis at his heels. When Justine crept in, she pulled the stone slab after her and propped it upright. The small aperture would be no more visible to prying eyes than it had been to her, who had knelt before the shrine so many times in prayer.

Denis paused when he came to the wider area, with Star Boy well ahead.

"Keep going!" Justine whispered urgently. "It's better farther on!" When they reached the chapel-like space with the pond, Star Boy bent to drink at the water and then stood up, grinning.

Denis stared around in astonishment. "I didn't know this was here! It's like a little house!"

"It is, but keep your voice down. They could be standing right over our heads, and there are cracks in the rocks—look at how the sun is shining through." She bent to return down the tunnel.

"Where are you going? You're not going to leave us?" Denis reached out to hold her.

"I must. I want to hear if they come down, and what they have to say. There's no danger here for you. Star Boy will look after you." As if he understood perfectly what she had said, the Indian boy came and stood over her brother, watching her exit solemnly.

It seemed that she lay waiting in the tunnel for ever, her body soaked and cramped. At last she heard voices over her head on the ridge top, still somewhat muffled by the rock barrier.

"Nothing my way. It was hard to see in the mist but maybe we'll find something now the sun is coming through."

"I've not had any luck, either"—that was the one called Philippe—"but there seems to be a path or two made through the forest." She knew who he was then: the tall gangly boy who trapped with his father beyond the village. He would know what to look for.

"They could have been there, then. Do you suppose there are any hiding-places down the cliff?"

It was what she had expected. She waited, knowing what was to come.

"Hey! I've found a path here! It's like steps down the cliff."

"Go down and we'll follow, Philippe."

"Watch your step!"

How strange they were, shouting away in the wilderness as if there were no dangers lurking. Philippe should have known better, even if the other two were farm boys. But perhaps they were shouting to keep their spirits up. Perhaps they were afraid—as she had been many times.

And then they sounded almost upon her. They had discovered the cave. There were more shouts, this time of triumph. Their voices echoed, distorted by the tunnel.

"What did I tell you? They've been here!"

"Look at these clothes. Are these human bones? Did they starve to death?"

"More likely taken by the Indians. There was a band of Iroquois here not so long ago. They've driven the Montagnais away."

"If they've been taken by the Iroquois, that's goodbye to them."

"He won't be pleased to hear that, but it was a wild goose chase anyway. How could two children, and one a girl, at that, survive in the wilderness this long?"

"Justine was no child. Since Michel went off, her father took her with him on all his trips to do wills and marriage contracts. And she looked after the whole St. Hilaire family when her mother was ill for so long after the last birth. She did it alone, too."

Who was that? It must be Henri, the Bergerons' boy, whom she had talked to at the mill. God bless him for defending her.

"Not so young, either, that he didn't have it in mind to marry her in a few years' time."

"He knows how to pick 'em, anyway. She's a pretty little thing." There came a pause. The voice when it came again had a strange quiver. "Or was. Look, let's get out of here. We've got what we want. But he's not going to be happy."

"Well, we are." That was Philippe again. "We've got the proof he wants that they've been stolen or worse. He or the others will have to pay us, and that means we're set up for our spring trip. Come on, let's go."

She had not realized how tense she had been lying in the tunnel until she heard them scramble up the cliff. It pained her to breathe and she tried to fill her lungs with air. As quickly as she could, she made her way back to the airy cave space and bathed her face and hands in the ice-cold water of the pond. Star Boy had been on the alert, watching the entry for her or anyone else to come.

Feeling free, they explored the underground world of the little chapel, examining the walls and the plants and insects that sheltered there. The pond seemed to have few occupants, only a few colourless fish and some spiders spinning on its surface.

Aware that the young men might still be above, they returned to their cave home in silence and quietly set about putting the place in order. By high noon all was silent above them and they ventured stealthily up the cliff to the ridge. There was no one in sight but a deer and her fawn browsing in a glade. Their domain was once again returned to them and the wild animals. In celebration they had a feast of moose meat and some black berries they had found where the deer had been grazing. Justine, in the evening, sang them a lullaby and told another story of King Dagobert, Star Boy listening as if he understood every word. For now all was well with her world. They had enough to eat and a place to hide. She would have to live day by day and wait for what came.

CHAPTER TEN

The Whales Have Come!

What came was so unexpected that it could have cost her her life. It was the following morning just after dawn and Justine was setting out early, before the boys had wakened, to fetch some kindling for the fire. As she climbed up the rocky trail and her eyes came level with the cliff edge, she nearly fell backwards in astonishment and fear. Only a few feet from her head were two brown legs, strong and sinewy, the legs of an Indian. Praise God his back was to her, and he had not heard her moving up the path! Hidden by the shrubs on the cliff face, she watched him. He was intent on something in the forest before him—an animal he hoped to trap? Another Indian he lay in wait for? Who was he? Could he be Star Boy's father or brother, come back to search for him? She could not take a chance that he was a friend, not in these forests. She waited, as still as a rabbit, and watched. Then she realized that he was listening. He had heard her on the cliff and did not know where the sound had come from! Swiftly, hardly daring to breathe, she descended the cliff trail and crept inside the cave.

The boys were still asleep and, as the sun came up and glowed in the river canyon, she waited for the sound that would tell her the Indian had followed her. But none came. An hour later she was warning them, Denis in words and Star Boy with gestures, that they could not leave the cave that day. She was thankful they had a good water supply and enough food to eat without lighting the fire. Surely if they waited for a few days, hidden in the cliff, he would be gone.

On the fourth day Justine decided that they must be safe. They needed water to drink and to refresh themselves in the continuing heat. She went first, wary of even the small animal sounds that rustled the undergrowth and last year's leaves and needles. She found no trace of the Indian. It seemed the forest had been returned to them. She felt a surge of relief flood her being. Whoever he was, friend or enemy, he had gone.

But her feeling of safety had come too soon. All three of them were drowsing behind a huge rock by the stream, their feet bathed in the cool water, when they saw a shadow slipping over the rock and along the forest path. They froze where they sat, their breath tight in their lungs. Then Star Boy crept out from behind their resting-place and beckoned them to follow.

When the figure finally came in sight they withdrew quickly into a huge tangle of tall ferns and waited. It was the Indian. He could only be the same one she had seen, his skin glistening in the half-dusk of the glade, a short knife gleaming in his hand. He turned as if to search the trail behind him and at that instant Justine felt Star Boy grow stiff and tense beside her. She looked at his face. For one so young its expression was astonishing, a violent mixture of fear and rage. Then she knew who this stranger was. No stranger to Star Boy—so he must be the Iroquois who had left him for dead. And he was capable, she knew, of killing them all. But why was he still here? Looking for another victim to torture and kill? Now he appeared to be on his way to the Montagnais village.

Following him, with footfalls as silent as his own, they found that this was indeed his goal. They watched from a thicket of young spruce while he made a methodical search of what remained in the village, tearing down the cache racks in the trees, enraged at finding nothing there, and scattering the burned debris around him as he swept over the site hunting for whatever booty he could find. They sensed his puzzlement as he searched, picking up only the odd fragment of tool or hide, a broken arrow or two. Then, as they watched, breathless, he made off in the direction he had come from, heading for a trail that led to the river. Doubtless his canoe was hidden in a cove at the base of the cliff. But they could not be sure. They dared not move. They waited, cramped and hungry, until dusk came, and then, aware that the forest had eyes on every path, they slipped back to the cave.

Not daring to light a fire, they ate cold food from their cache, keeping their conversation to whispers. But there was no sound above them in the forest, no creak of boughs bending to a human body. Now and then Star Boy, rigid with expectation, crept out to listen. At one point she saw him pick up a large rock and hold it tightly in his hand. But she knew there would be no hope in that if the Indian found them. What good were rocks against a knife and a tall, strong body? They were only children, defenceless against an enemy who had already tried to kill one of them. Justine could imagine his rage if he discovered his victim was still alive. What their fate would be, she dared not consider. But the dusk turned into night and no one came. The loons were calling again on the water below, a fox was barking in the forest, a companionable owl swooped into their cave to find a hideaway to devour a mouse, and that was all. Worn out with the day's events, when the stars shone on the great river Saguenay they fell asleep.

She wakened with a tremor in the night, aware that something had startled her, nerves ever alert for danger. Had the Indian found them at last? Breathing a prayer, she lay rigid, opening her eyes only enough to catch a glimpse of the cave entrance before her. *It was Star Boy! What was he doing? Moving outside to get some air in the stifling night? But no, he was creeping towards her place on her rock bed!* Only when she saw him reach out a cautious hand did she remember. Before she had lain down to sleep, perspiring with heat and anxiety, she had for the first time removed the ruby red necklace from her neck and placed it on the stone slab beside her. She was cooler without it clinging to her skin. She guessed at once what he was about. She knew how the Indians treasured the brightly coloured beads that the traders often gave in exchange for furs. Perhaps he thought he might use it as a charm against the evil of his Indian enemy, or in barter for his life.

Scarcely daring to breathe, she watched him draw closer. He knelt beside the stone slab and slowly reached out his small hand to touch the colourful beads that shone even in the dim light of the cave. Lightly he ran his fingers around the circlet, his eyes glowing like the beads. Then, with a deep sigh that seemed to fill the cave with its echo, he withdrew his hand. Still kneeling, he kept his eyes on the necklace for what seemed to her an eternity. Then he crept away to his own rock and spruce-bough bed without a backward glance. Tears flowed down her cheeks in gratitude. In the morning the necklace was still there.

The image of the Indian with the knife scarcely left her thoughts in the week following, until another took its place. It began with Denis calling to her from where he stood on the ledge looking down on the great river. "Justine! Justine, there's smoke on the water! Come and see!"

Smoke? What could that mean? She hastened to his side and looked where he was pointing. Away down the river, where the wide waters of the Saguenay flowed to join those of the St. Lawrence, strange puffs of vapour came and went in the hot, still air.

"Denis! It's the whales! The whales have come!"

She knew what that meant. The month of August was well past the half-way point and the autumn was nearly upon them. Every year they waited for the whales. Although they were sighted earlier in the year, the greatest gathering of them arrived towards the middle and end of August, when they came to feed on the underwater life where the two mighty rivers met. Every year the people of the settlement had watched the massive bodies gliding in and out of the water like ships that did not have to sail on the surface. She had heard they were friendly creatures, swimming alongside the fishermen's boats or even beneath them, but they too were among the hunted. Whalers from the Basque country had come, even before the settlers, seeking the riches to be made from their oil and flesh.

It was the small white ones Justine liked best, the belugas, playing in family groups where the two strong tides overlapped one another. But today the spouts were too far away for her to see what kind of whales they were.

"Does that mean summer's nearly over?" Denis's question seemed innocent enough but it made her shiver.

"Yes, nearly over." She said no more, her heart heavy with decisions to be made.

With the whales here, it could only be a matter of days before they saw the long skeins of geese high over them in the sky, honking and crying their mournful farewell to summer on their way south. And what of Denis, Star Boy, and herself? Where could they go?

About this time at home she and Denis would have been helping Papa prepare the cabin for winter, packing earth and straw around the stone foundation to keep out the frost and the cold. And Papa would have been getting his wood ready for the winter carving he did by the fire. She recalled with a pain at her heart how, the year before he died, he had carved a statue of the Blessed Virgin and Child for the church, and Maman had embroidered a cloth for the altar.

She remembered the only trip she had ever been on at the height of winter. Papa had had to go up the river ice to a tiny settlement that had no scribe to draw up a marriage contract. She had gone with him in the sledge pulled by their team of oxen, a chunk of frozen bean porridge tied to the back and a pot of burning coals for fuel. Papa had taken his goose feather to dip in boiled maple bark for his inscribing, and sand for blotting. After the signing there had been a wonderful betrothal party with feasting and dancing all night long, before they had set off for home again. On the return journey Papa had done some work for an innkeeper and they had stayed a night with him. She had been piled in a bed of leaves with two strange women for company, covered only with a deerskin.

But all of that was luxury compared to what lay ahead of them here in the forest. She knew that winter, not the Iroquois, was their greatest enemy after all. Soon the two immense rivers would be sheets of ice and the ships from faraway France would come no more until spring. And what of their clothing? It was becoming more threadbare every day. Even Star Boy could not help them survive in the blinding snow and deadly cold. In their own log cabin in the days that now seemed so long ago, it had been impossible to keep warm when there was frost on the homespun blankets every morning, and ice in the water jug. In a village winter in New France there was no sound of revelry in the streets, only sometimes the crackle of sledge runners on the snow, the jingle of bells, and the sharp retort of the trees in the forest cracking with frost, a sound like gunfire.

As she lay awake, looking out at the stars, long after the two boys were asleep, she recalled a terrible story brought by their neighbour Roger Collet on his return from a journey upriver. He told of a priest travelling in the winter to visit a mission several leagues away. He had been found a month later, a statue on his knees, frozen to death in the snow.

Were the whales a sign to her that she should give up and find her way back to the village? Should she make her way, with the two boys, to the shore of the St. Lawrence and find a ship that would take the three of them to Quebec and the convent? Perhaps she could try to be another Sister Marie of the Incarnation. They had all heard of Sister Marie working like a saint to care for the Indians, nursing them through smallpox, teaching them devotion to Jesus and the Blessed Virgin. In Quebec there were sisters of God in the hospital and in the convent. They would never turn Star Boy away.

The crack of thunder, when it came, jolted her awake and to her feet. Denis cried in his sleep and she bent to comfort him. Star Boy slept on as if nothing would wake him. She went out to look at the sky. The massed clouds and the scud almost touched the hilltop above her. Lightning sizzled down the canyon of the river and dropped in flaming balls into the water. Then the rain came, torrents of it, slashing down the face of the cliff and onto the ledge where she stood, washing away the humid sweat of weeks past. Her clothes were soaked and her hair streaming, but she did not care. With the fresh wind came a renewal of hope. There was a change in the weather; there could be a change in their fortunes.

As she stood in the downpour listening to the trees cracking and snapping in the tumult of wind, another bolt of lightning split the sky. It was then she saw the figure, standing as she stood in the storm, but on the opposite river shore. She thought she might have imagined her vision, confusing it with a dead tree trunk, but no—the lightning flared again down on the river and the figure was still there. And was that a canoe drawn up on the rocks beside him? Perhaps it was a *coureur de bois* on his way home from the forest, possibly someone who could help them when the morning light came. Oh, if only he wouldn't disappear! But then, it could be an Indian, part of an advance party exploring the way before an attack on the village—perhaps the very Iroquois they had evaded a week ago! Swinging between hope and despair, she took off her soaked outer clothing, rolled up in her old cloak and went in to sleep. She watched the lightning playing around the cave entrance, heard the thunder rumbling away into the wilderness with a sound like far Indian drums, but imprinted on her mind's eye was a black figure silhouetted against rock and water far below.

She warned Denis of him in the morning and, with mime, tried to tell Star Boy. Then they were all happy to sit by the warmth of the fire. The cold winds that now swept down the river canyon and up the huge cliffs were the first warning of autumn. Later, as they set forth to find more food on the ridge, she looked for traces of the first colour among the clump of hardwoods they passed through on the way to the stream. She knew the trees there would soon look like the multi-coloured ribbons that decked the maypole in the village square every first of May.

All day, with the spectre of winter hovering at her shoulder, she kept going out to the ledge to seek signs of the figure on the river. Could it be Jean-Luc, he of the noisy oaths and pockmarked face, come in search of her? Had he guessed her disguise? But that was ridiculous. Jean-Luc was far up the Saguenay with his fellows, hunting for furs or bartering for them with trade goods in some friendly Indian encampment. Just the same, she would have to be careful. *Coureur* or Indian, either could mean disaster.

The next day was warmer, the sun blazing in a sky of brilliant blue. Star Boy disappeared in mid-morning and came back with a duck he had caught in a snare. They roasted it for their noon meal and then he hung the webbed feet and beak around his neck on a hide thong. He looked very pleased with himself.

"Why does he do that?" Denis asked. "For good luck?"

"For good luck and good fishing. Remember Papa telling us about the Indians who came to the fort with bears' claws and foxes' teeth hung about their bodies, so they would be brave like the bear or cunning like the fox?"

Denis eyed her wistfully. "Can't we hang something around our necks so we can go home?"

"We shall go. I know we shall."

"Do you mean that? Truly?"

"Of course." But her promises were hollow, she knew that. Unless she resolved to sacrifice herself—and she knew the time was approaching when she had to make up her mind to do just that.

"Star Boy will come with us, won't he?"

"What a silly question!" She cuffed him lightly on his hair. "We could never let him go. He's one of our family." Sent to us to make up for other losses, she thought.

With nuts and berries ripening, with roots and mushrooms and fresh green plants still in abundance and moose meat hanging in the cave, they had no need to go hungry. As the days grew warmer a sense of security again seemed to surround them. If the weather would stay just like this, she thought, we could live here for ever, children of the wilderness together. True, their clothing was falling apart with daily use and soon they would have to resort to deer or moosehide cover-ups, but what of that? Star Boy would make some for them.

As she was planning and daydreaming at the mouth of the cave, she looked up and, high on the opposite ridge, she saw smoke. Indians! It *had* been an Indian she had seen down on the river. The Iroquois had returned! Her dreams vanished. Now what should she do? She hesitated to tell the others until she was sure.

Denis's mind was on other things after the evening meal. "Do you think we'll ever have little sweet cakes again?" he asked.

"Lots of them." She forced a laugh. "If we stay here long enough, I might find out how to make them of ground roots and tree sap!" *If only we live*, she thought. *If we're not taken by Iroquois.*

CHAPTER ELEVEN

"There's somebody up there!"

Her mind was far from cakes the next day. It was early morning, and she had had to warn Star Boy of the smoke across the river before he slipped away again to hunt with his hand-crafted bow and arrows. She knew something was wrong when the first violent pains racked her body. What was it? Some terrible disease that had caught up with her in the stress of wilderness living? A poison come from who knew where? Then she remembered that her breakfast portion of moose meat had had a strange sour taste. She had spoken of it to Denis but he had devoured his with no qualms and apparently no evil results. It was her piece only, then. It must not have been properly cured.

With a cry she rushed from the cave and vomited at the rim of the ledge. Denis stood by in horror, helplessly watching his sister retching again and again until there was not an ounce of strength left in her.

"Denis, bring me water," she whispered. "I need water."

"But there isn't any!" Appalled, he stared at her lying on the cave floor. "This was the day you were going to the river to get water."

"There's none at all?"

"Not a drop. We used the last to heat the moose meat this morning."

"But I can't wait until Star Boy comes back! I can't breathe! Oh, Denis, I feel so ill!"

"Then I'll go!"

"You?" She tried to struggle up on her elbow. "Alone?"

"I have to." His face wore an odd look of astonishment, as if he had surprised himself. "I *have* to go, if you need water and Star Boy isn't here."

She tried to reach out to clasp him to her. "Oh, Denis, why did I ever get you into this? Why?"

"You didn't. I came myself." He pulled away from her resolutely. "And now I can go myself. I'll take the caribou-leg skin and two gourds and try to fill them all."

She lay struggling to breathe, and to stifle the waves of nausea.

"You'll be careful, won't you? Go one step at a time, and listen." She recalled the smoke and the figure in the night on the opposite shore. "Oh, Denis, do go softly and keep your eyes and ears open!"

Without another word or a backward glance he began to climb the cliff face. She waited, her prayers mingling with the nausea and bouts of retching. She looked with horror at her stained clothing. It was already in tatters, as careful as she had been, and now this!

Suddenly she heard him on the downward path again. Coming back so soon? Her heart beat wildly until she thought it would burst through her threadbare shirt. "Denis, is that you?" she whispered.

"Yes." He slipped softly into the cave, his face ashen. "There's somebody up there!"

"Somebody? An Iroquois?"

"I don't know. I don't think so. He was bending low to stare at the ground as if he was looking for something. All I could see were his legs, but they had clothes on!"

She sank back, exhausted. "One of Louis Gaudin's friends, then. Was it someone we know?"

"I don't think so. When he bent down I could see a brown beard."

"A brown beard? Mathieu Trudel has a brown beard and he's a friend of Louis Gaudin's." And she had thought they were safe after Henri Bergeron and his friends had found the clothing. "He was searching for traces of our having been there, that's what he was doing." A wave of intense weakness overcame her. She was silent.

Gently Denis reached out a hand and touched her burning forehead. "Justine, I can get water."

"But you can't. If he sees you, whoever he is, that means the end of everything!" And then she thought, *and maybe it's for the best*. Maybe she would have to give in and admit that she had lost her fight for her own way of life.

"But nobody will see me! I know where I can get water and nobody will ever see me!"

"Where?"

"From the pond at the end of the tunnel behind the little shrine—I can fill the skin and gourds there!"

"Denis, I never thought of that!" A new hope surged through her. "There is water there, of course." She eyed him with doubt. "You don't mind crawling there alone? You wouldn't be frightened?"

He tried to stand tall, his small shoulders squared. "Why should I be? There's nothing in there to hurt me." Even so, his face looked bleak.

She wept for joy. "Oh, Denis, Denis, thank you! I'm so very thirsty!"

"I'm going now." He tried to smooth her matted hair. "Don't be worried. You'll be better, just see if you're not, when I bring the water."

Carefully he moved the stone slab that guarded the entrance to the tunnel and then, the skin and gourds clutched tight against his chest, he began his difficult crawl with only one swift, anxious backward glance.

It seemed an eternity before she heard the measured crunch of knee after knee on the tunnel floor again, and then there he was, his small face glowing with triumph, holding the containers aloft. "I had to put them down each time I crawled so they wouldn't spill. But there's water here. Lots of it!"

"Oh, praise God! Thank you, thank you, Denis!" She reached out to grab the caribou skin, but Denis held it tight.

"You mustn't drink too quickly. Remember when Maman had such a bout and she nearly died? Michel said she must have only a spoonful at a time."

"Yes, I remember. I'll be careful, I promise. Give me only a sip, and then another."

Denis held the skin so that the cold beautiful water flowed gently into her mouth. She longed for great gulps but held herself back, taking slow swallows every few moments. It was as if she were sitting down to a banquet. She felt she could have fainted with weakness without the water, and never had liquid tasted so wonderful. After an hour of sipping and craving more, she drifted into a sound sleep.

When she wakened, the shadows on the cave floor told her that the day was well advanced. Star Boy and Denis knelt beside her, watching her every breath. But Star Boy held something in his hand, a tiny leaf container of light brown liquid. He held it to her lips and, trusting, she drank slowly. It had a sweet nutty taste, a brew made, no doubt, from the sap of some tree with health-giving qualities. Star Boy would know. With the sweetness came more strength and a knowledge that she was, after all, going to go on living.

In a kind of pleasant daze she lay on the cave floor and watched the boys prepare supper. Star Boy had caught another rabbit and the aroma of its cooking did not sicken her as she thought it would, but she did not eat. There were more sips from the nutty sap, and quiet moments inside the cave when she managed to ask Star Boy in signs if he had seen the intruder, but the answer was a shake of the head and a puzzled frown. Wherever he was, he had, she hoped, left their own cave area, so that she need not live in constant fear.

She slept again, this time through the long night, waking to the late dawn of early autumn. She wondered why she did not feel cold, and then realized that Denis had covered her with her old cloak. She knew, too, that her strength was returning, and she even ventured to swallow a little shredded rabbit along with the nutty sap that Star Boy seemed to have in constant supply.

In the few days that it took her to return to her old self, the boys took over the management of daily life in the cave. Mimicking Star Boy, Denis helped with the meals, fetched more water from the inner cave, and kept their wilderness home in a reasonable state of tidiness. He watched over Justine like a mother hen over her chick, forbidding her to eat too much at a time, keeping her ragged clothing sponged and clean, and helping her out to the massive bushes beyond the cave when the need arose.

On the fourth day she knew she must go to the river to bathe. "Oh, Denis, I smell as bad as that meat I ate!" she complained. "I have to go!"

"Then I'll come with you."

"Not this time. I'll be all right. You stay with Star Boy because I want to get right into the water, and I don't want him there." She wondered why she should feel such prudery after all this time, but privacy of her person was of profound importance to her.

"You'll be careful, won't you?"

"I shall be. I promise. After all, you and Star Boy have been up in the forest together and seen no one. I think he's gone, whoever he was. Given up, I hope."

She managed to get to the river and, casting her remnants of clothing aside, rejoiced in the shock of crystal-clear water. She even lingered for a moment to watch the beaver at work once more on a winter home. But her peace was short-lived. She was almost back at the cliff's edge when she heard voices.

"Lean on me. Let the other foot bear the weight."

"Praise God you were here. I'd never have made it back to the village without some help."

"How did it happen?"

"It was a fool's mistake, or a coward's. I don't know which."

"No need to blame yourself." The voice was deep, concerned, kind. "Were you running?"

"Yes, I thought I needed to. I saw a lone Indian coming up the cliff. I didn't wait to find out if he was Montagnais or Iroquois, and he could have been one of many. It was a good distance back there, at the bend in the river. As soon as I saw him I shot through the forest like a greased pig and fell right into a porcupine's hole among the rocks. Do you think the ankle's broken?"

"Perhaps only sprained. I've bound it tightly with birchbark. I'll tend it better when we get back to the village." The deeper voice took on an air of puzzlement. "But why are you up here alone?"

"I could ask the same thing of you. Searching for the missing two. A different kind of hunt, that's sure."

"There's more in this for me, you know that. You shouldn't risk your life alone when there's already been an Iroquois raid here."

"You're doing the same, even if your reward would be greater."

The deep voice was filled with a fierce determination. "I'll find them if it takes me a year!"

"Or their bones. Will you be satisfied then?"

"Don't speak so." The tone was harsh, almost violent. "I'll find them, I tell you, and confound all the know-it-alls!"

"Well, the others found the clothes. I thought I'd have one more try, but this is the end for me. I can see it isn't for you, though."

The voices began to fade into the distance, muffled by light winds and wild growth. "As long as there's any doubt at all I'll...." But what the speaker intended was lost on the forest trail.

Justine had seen neither one, safely hidden as she was behind a huge and tightly knit glade of alder trees, but she had heard every word. So that was it. Louis Gaudin was never going to give up; he was still offering rewards for her capture, richer rewards than ever, if she could believe what she'd heard. They would never be safe. She felt a surge of hopelessness. The only solution was to escape farther up the Saguenay, farther from the village and the searchers. Could Star Boy help them survive in the terrible conditions that lay ahead? There was another answer, she knew, but she hardly dared admit it. She could let Star Boy and Denis run free, to be found by the villagers—and go on alone herself.

She would have to decide soon. Each encounter was closer than the last. She thought of Louis Gaudin and shuddered, and came to her decision swiftly. That was what she would do. If she explained to Denis that he and

Star Boy must find a path back to the village and safety, and leave her to go on alone, that would be the answer.

In the cave, when the autumn dark had fallen as swiftly as a bat's wing, she dared to tell him. Star Boy was watching, his eyes intent, aware. "I think one of them was Mathieu Trudel, Denis. So that means they're still searching. I want to go on alone and send you back to safety. Star Boy will lead you to Tadoussac, I know he will. He's learned to trust us now and he knows all the forest trails."

Denis stared at her, dismayed. "And what will happen to us when we get there?"

"The Jesuit fathers will look after you, or the priest. I know they will. The Blessed Virgin will see to it."

"What about you? What will you do?"

"I'll go down to the river shore and wait for a friendly brigade to come down the Saguenay." She spoke with a cheerful confidence she did not feel. "There'll be more *coureurs de bois* coming home for the winter. They'll hide me until another sailing ship comes from France and then I'll try to board it secretly to go upriver to the convent nuns. There may even be some on the ship."

Denis's cry rang through the cave, causing a look of alarm on Star Boy's face. "But I don't want to go!"

"You'll be safe with Star Boy, I promise you. He's never let us down yet."

"It isn't that." She saw him suddenly stand straight and tall. "We can't leave you alone, to be taken by the Iroquois or eaten by the wolves. I want to stay to protect you!"

Moved, she stared at him, tears filling her eyes. "Oh, Denis, how you've grown! You want to protect me?"

"Oh, yes, please don't send us away! I could never be happy. I'd never know what had happened to you!"

Suddenly she made up her mind. She gathered him to her in a swift embrace and reached out to touch Star

Boy on the shoulder. "Very well. We'll all go together. Farther up the river. Somehow we shall live."

"When? When shall we go?"

"In the early morning tomorrow. Just before sunrise. It's too dangerous in the darkness and almost as dangerous in the light of day."

With gestures and pictures on the cave floor, they told Star Boy what they intended. He had no difficulty understanding, and before they slept they gathered their pitiful belongings in Justine's cloak and the moosehide and tried to return the cave floor to its former natural state, so that if anyone came that way there would be no telltale evidence of their occupation.

The boys slept at once, but Justine lay awake far into the night, wondering about the wisdom of her decision. It was a selfish one, she knew that, because of her loathing of Louis Gaudin. She knelt and asked forgiveness of the Blessed Virgin and prayed for blessings on their journey. Only then did she, too, sleep.

The cry of some night animal wakened her before the dark began to fade, and they ate a hasty breakfast and prepared to climb the cliff. She was going first, treading lightly and carefully, the others at her heels, when, with a tug that nearly sent her sprawling down the cliffside, Star Boy caught hold of her foot. She looked down, startled. His hand was on his mouth. *What had he heard?* She waited, moving not an inch, and still Star Boy did not stir. Then she heard it: the crackle of a twig, the soft whisper of clothing brushing undergrowth. Someone was coming! An Iroquois warrior, the same who had come before, the hated enemy of Star Boy? But if there was clothing brushing the undergrowth it couldn't be an Indian, who would most likely still be wearing only a breechcloth at this time of year. The man with the deep voice, then—the one who had been helping the wounded searcher back to the village. He would have had time to reach there and return. And how determined he must be to find his quarry, if he was up on the ridge this early in the morning! *They were trapped.* She felt sudden total despair. All the sacrifice and hardship they had endured to make her escape to freedom and a new life had been to no avail. If he stayed in the neighbourhood for long they would be prisoners in their own secret place, without the possibility of hunting for food. Perhaps if they waited until nightfall, their luck would be better. They would try again one more time, and that was all. Silently she motioned them down the cliff face and just as silently they returned to the cave and set about laying out food and water, ready for the long wait.

They said little, conversing in whispers and gestures, too alert to danger even to play a quiet game.

Denis leaned close to her. "Who could the other one be, Justine? If the first one was Mathieu Trudel, who was the other?"

"Another friend of Monsieur Gaudin's. You may be sure of that. Perhaps even a relative come from France."

"There was one coming, he told me that when you'd gone. A cousin, I think." Denis frowned, bewildered. "But why would even a cousin want to help him if he's as bad as you say he is?"

"Because they don't know that he isn't a good, honourable person. Some day I'll explain, Denis. Some day when we are safe, and far from here and him. For now, please believe me, I can't go back to Louis Gaudin."

Denis looked surprisingly wise. "Maybe Monsieur Gaudin promised this new man some land if he found us. That plot he owns up beyond the fort. I heard him boasting about getting it cheap from Monsieur Favreau's widow one day."

"You did? Madame Favreau needed money desperately, I know that. She wanted to go back to France and start a new life. And he got it cheap, you say?"

"For next to nothing, after he had a quiet talk with her. What did he mean by that?"

"It could mean anything. That's the answer, then. A plot of land like that is worth a dangerous search for two runaways. But whoever is looking for us, Denis, they won't find us. They won't, I swear it!"

It was as if Star Boy heard the anxiety and tears in her voice. He reached down, picked up the crude bow and arrow he had used to kill so much of their game, and came to stand beside her. She felt a deep sense of comfort. He had spoken in his own silent way.

Dusk came at last and she knew that, with the food almost gone, they could not put off leaving any longer. "I'll go first," she told them quietly. "Watch me from the rim of the cliff and be ready to slip down again if need be. Only come when I wave."

It was at the hour of the night when an uncanny stillness invades the forest, as if the wild things are waiting for some kind of signal to assure them that it is safe to venture forth to seek water at the river's edge, or food.

She went as swiftly as an animal herself up to the cliff's edge. Sensing nothing beyond her in the darkness, she crawled warily on hands and knees, hidden by the foliage and yet with a view of the immediate area around the vicinity of the cave.

"I think, little one, that you and I have been playing a grand game of hide-and-seek."

The voice almost sickened her with shock and surprise. It was the deep one again, the one belonging to the hunter who was determined to search for a year to find them. She saw the Indian moccasins first, then the deerskin gaiters at eye level, embroidered with symbols of travel. Above them were canvas trousers with supple leather at the knees, a scarlet jerkin, and on his head a fur headband with a coon tail trailing to the shoulder.

Even in the darkness she could see that he stood as still as the trees that sheltered him. But he was staring at her with piercing blue eyes set in a weather-tanned face. It was all up with them now. This was the end of escape, of hiding. Her grasp went suddenly to the ruby red necklet inside her ragged shirt and she prayed a silent, desperate cry to the Blessed Virgin. Then she waited for a hand to fall.

"Little one, don't you know me?"

Know him? A friend, then? Someone from the village sent to search for them with good intent? She tried to recall the voice without success. Whoever he was, she hoped he would treat them with kindness. An unbearable weight seemed to roll from her shoulders. She could do nothing more. Whatever life held now, she would have to trust to God. Again she waited, crouched at the feet of the stranger.

A strong hand reached down and gently lifted her to her feet. "Little sister, have you forgotten me so soon?"

Sister! Little sister! Could it really be Michel? This stranger with the skin baked almost black by sun and wind, and the crisp nut-brown beard and the man's figure standing tall and broad-shouldered? Was this the boy who had crept away in the night? Even his voice had changed, grown richer and deeper with his years in the wilderness. Little wonder she had taken it for a stranger's!

Then she saw the sudden sweet smile and she knew him. *Michel!* She flung herself into his arms in a torrent of weeping, "Oh, Michel, you've come! Praise all the saints and the Holy Mother! They sent you here!"

He held her so close she could scarcely breathe. His voice when it came was no more than a whisper. "It took effort and prayers of my own, little one. You seemed determined to escape me. I've been up and down the river for a week searching for you!"

"But how did you know where to find us? We've been hidden for so long. How did you know?"

Michel held her away from him and planted a loving kiss on the top of her fair head. "There are many tales to be told, Justine." He held her close again in another warm embrace. "But all that matters now is that you are safe. And Denis, too?"

"Oh yes, and our friend Star Boy, as well. Come! I'll show you our home in the wilderness."

She saw the radiant light of the full moon break over the treetops as they made their way down the cliff. "And I want to know, sweet child," Michel said, "how you came to it and why."

CHAPTER TWELVE

A Voyager Returns

With a rush of joy she led him to the ledge and into the cave.

"But where have they gone?" She stared around in amazement. There was no sign of either Denis or Star Boy. "I know!" She raced to the end of the cave and moved the stone slab. "Denis, it's all right! You and Star Boy can come out!"

"He's hiding? In there?"

"Oh, yes. We've used it before. It goes away back under the rocks." She shouted again down the rock tunnel. "Denis! Don't be afraid. It's Michel, our brother, Michel! He's come back! He's here!"

They heard a scuffle inside the rock and Denis's face appeared at the opening. He looked at the brown-bearded face in fright. "That's not Michel!" He tried to put on a brave front. "Is it truly?"

"Truly it is! It is! Come out, you'll see for yourself!"

He came out slowly, keeping well back from this stranger in *coureur* garb. "I never saw him before."

"Not as I am now, Denis." Michel reached out and drew him gently to his side. "But over two years have passed. I went away a boy and I came back a man. No wonder you don't know me. I hardly know you, you've grown so!"

He hugged the boy to him in a swift gesture. "And I discover you're all I have left to come home to."

"But there's Star Boy, too. Without him we wouldn't be here. Is he in the tunnel, Denis?"

"No. We heard voices while we waited, and when we crept out to look, we saw you there with"—he looked up uncertainly—"with *him*. And Star Boy went faster than I've ever seen him go. He raced up the cliff on the other side of the cave."

"He ran away?" Justine looked at the hiding-place as if she did not believe him.

"Right away, without a sound."

Michel looked from one to the other, puzzled. "Who is this, this Star Boy, who seems to mean so much to you? Did someone come with you from the village?"

"Oh no, he was waiting for us here in the forest. He's a Montagnais Indian, a little younger than me. The Iroquois came and burned his village and then they left him here to die." Justine remembered the scene they had found and shuddered.

"How did they do that?" Michel drew them out onto the ledge and sat down.

Denis broke in quickly. "They had him all tied down with thongs and stakes. I thought he was dead when we found him. *I* found him," he added proudly. "We named him after a little friend of Papa's that you never knew."

"They did this to a child?" Michel frowned. "That surely must have been an act of individual vengeance. Even Iroquois take children from other tribes and adopt them as their own."

"That's what I thought. But he knows all about living in the wild, Michel. He brought us food and made us extra clothing from the hides of animals we snared. He

even prepared a moose calf so we could have meat!"
Justine pointed inside the cave, lit by moonlight. "See?
There's still a little smoked meat left hanging from the
cave ceiling. We forgot it when we were cleaning the
cave before we were to leave!"

"And he's Montagnais?" There was a strange air
of puzzlement about Michel, a questioning lift of the
eyebrows.

"Oh, yes." Justine spoke with certainty. "The village
was burned almost to the ground, but we found tools and
cooking utensils and a knife!" She flourished it proudly.
"And there were storage racks up in the trees."

"Where food for the winter was hidden to keep it safe
from animals and the enemy." Michel smiled. "You see,
I know."

Justine flung her arms about his neck again. "You
know because you lived like an Indian. But you've come
back to us! You've come back!" Then anxiety clouded
her face. "But what about Star Boy? Will he come back?
Oh, he must! He just has to!"

"I think he's probably very close now, watching and
listening to see if you're in any danger." Michel glanced
to the cliff top. "He'll come back, I'm sure of it."

For the first time, real joy shone on Denis's face.
"Does that mean we can go back too, back home? Is that
what it means?"

"That and much more, Denis," Michel said.

Justine sat close to him, as if she was afraid he would
disappear like a puff of smoke from the campfire. "But
how did you come at all? Tell us everything, Michel!"

"Not before I hear your story. I'll tell you this much. I
came expecting to find a loving family to welcome me,
and I found no one." He drew them close, an arm around
each shoulder. "Our friends in the settlement told me
what had happened that night in the cabin. It was a spark
from the hearth, they thought."

"Yes, a spark from the hearth." Justine hid her face.

"Can you bear to tell me what happened then?"

She told him, hearing again the roar of the flames, the screams of the animals in the barn, and reliving the agony of their loss.

"How could I be away when you needed me most?" Michel said.

"That was God's blessing, Michel. It was Denis who thought of it. If you'd been home you would have been trapped in the loft." She searched his face for an answer. "But how did you know to come here?"

"It seems Gervaise tried to look after you."

"Yes, and he didn't come back. That's why we had to come up here."

"He didn't come back because he fell from the scaffold while he was helping Robert Lavigne build his barn and broke his leg. He's able to hobble about on crutches now."

She heard the news with relief and joy. Gervaise had not deserted them after all.

"He hoped you'd return to the village," Michel went on. "He was prepared to fight your case and get you away from your trouble. When there was no sign of you returning or in the place where he'd last seen you, he persuaded some of the young men of the village—three of them, I think—to come in search of you. His family promised to help outfit them for a trader's voyage in the spring if they found you."

"Henri Bergeron from the mill was one! I know, I heard them! I thought Louis Gaudin had sent them."

"That wretch! Why did they ever let him take you in? Papa never trusted him. Did he harm you?" Michel looked fierce.

"No, oh no! But I knew I couldn't stay. They were even talking of my marrying him in a few years' time!"

"Thanks be to God I'm home!" Michel said. "It was Gervaise who set me on the right trail. He told me Henri and the others had brought back your clothes but he knew you were in his brother Marc's clothing, and that meant you could still be about the cave they described. But they couldn't tell me where it was. There are hundreds of caves along the Saguenay!"

"Then how did you find this one?" Denis wanted to know.

"I have been up and down the river a dozen times searching for you, watching the cliffs for any sign of movement. A few days ago I was sure I saw someone up here, so I stayed in the area. There was a terrible storm and in the lightning I thought I saw a small figure up here on the rocks."

"And I saw you! I saw you!" Justine cried out.

"And now we're together again," Michel said. "But what a place to seek shelter. In the wilderness!"

"Star Boy helped us. Without him we'd be gone." Justine stood up and stared at the cliff trail. "You really do think he'll come back, don't you?"

"I do. Just be patient and wait. He must learn to trust me here and to know I mean you no harm. Nor him either."

But even after the late supper they ate at the fire Michel kindled, there was still no sign of Star Boy. Justine wondered how he was faring alone in the forest. *He must come back! If not, they would go in search of him.*

Michel saw the anxiety in her eyes. "Don't fret now. Just have faith, the kind that has kept you alive all these many weeks, and you'll see him again."

"Then will you tell us your adventures, Michel?" Denis was sleepy, but not too sleepy to listen.

"Adventures! I've had enough to last a lifetime!" Michel stared into the flames, remembering.

"You went away with Simon Guillet's crew, didn't you?"

"Yes. There were four of us." He bowed his head and crossed himself. "I'm the only one who came back."

There was silence for a long moment. "Was it the Iroquois?" Justine asked quietly.

"Not this time, Justine. There are other dangers in the wilderness besides Iroquois. We travelled far away from any settlement, hoping to make contact with some Indian band who would give us furs for our few trade goods. By autumn we had a small hoard but we decided to hold on until spring, hoping to grow rich if we got more furs farther north." Michel shivered. "The winter was the worst I have ever seen. Sometimes we had to dig a hole in the snow and cover it with spruce and cedar branches and then pile more snow on top to keep from freezing. And many times our food ran out and we had to eat lichens and bark to stay alive."

"We ate wild plants and roots when we first came," Justine told him. "We still eat them. Star Boy knows which ones are best. He's found them for us."

"Ah yes, but in winter it's hard to find even those."

Justine looked at him lovingly. "Michel, I'll make a supper for you fit for the King of France himself when we go home!" Then she remembered that there was no home to go to. But home would be where Michel was, and Denis, and Star Boy.

"See that you do. The biggest *tourtière* in New France! Mind you, the villagers have spoiled me since I got home. Every day has been like a feast day, with all our friends bringing something."

"But when the spring came the wild plants grew again," Denis put in, "and you could get roots from the ground."

"True," Michel agreed. "Just as well, after we had chewed on our moccasins for food. But then came the mosquitoes and little black flies. They almost ate us alive!"

"We've had them here, too," Justine said. "We couldn't even make a smoke fire to drive them away, for fear of telling someone where we were." She showed him the bites on her arm. "Star Boy had leaves he rubbed on them. The same way he treated Denis's wound."

"Denis was hurt?" Michel pulled his brother to him. "What's this?" Briefly they told him how it had happened, and how Star Boy had come to the rescue. But Denis wanted to hear more of Michel's story. "What about when the spring came? Did you go farther into the wilderness? Did you have more adventures?"

"Too many," Michel said wryly. "Too many. There were times when a quiet river ran into rapids or a storm blew up on a lake and we had to leap into the water to save the canoes. Sometimes we were on the edge of a waterfall before we knew it was there, and we had to rescue our trade goods and supplies and drag them soaking to the shore."

"But did you find many furs?" Denis wanted to know.

"Some, and those of good quality we got from the Algonkian tribes. Sometimes we got a beautiful beaver pelt for just a needle, a looking-glass, or a string of beads. But we sold the furs to other traders for more trade goods, knives, blankets, trinkets, because we wanted to explore farther."

"And what did you find there?" Denis asked. "Papa used to tell us that a fine adventurer might find a way to the east, where gold and spices are."

"Those we did not find, Denis. The winter came again, with ice and snow and hungry days and nights. Then one day we were trying to cross a lake on our snowshoes to set up traps. But the sun had softened the ice and snow and François fell through."

Justine asked softly, "Did he drown?"

"Yes, and later so did all the others. We were trying to navigate a huge lake in the canoes but a storm came up with waves like mountains. It came on suddenly. We never had a chance!" It seemed as if Michel was blaming himself for what had happened. "I was the only one who made it to shore, clinging to an overturned canoe." He bowed his head and crossed himself again. "God rest their souls."

"And God be thanked you came back to us," Justine said fervently. "There must be more to the story. What did you do alone?"

"The 'more' will have to wait until tomorrow," Michel decided. "It's time you went to sleep."

"But I can't sleep until Star Boy comes back," Justine protested. "I'll sit here on the ledge, feeling safe now that you're here, Michel."

"No, you will sleep, both of you," Michel said firmly. "If he hasn't come back by the morning, we'll go into the forest to search for him."

"Then we'll pray first," Justine said, just as firmly. "We have our own shrine in the cave."

They went in and knelt before it, pouring forth their thanks for Michel's return and their own safety. "And, Blessed Ones, watch over Star Boy, wherever he is! Keep him safe from the wild animals and bring him back to us soon!" Justine clutched the ruby red necklace in her hands. It was her link with home and all that had been, her promise for the future.

Later, as she lay watching the stars shining beyond the cave entrance, she thought she heard a sound, no more than the rustle of a mole on the forest floor. Quickly she crept to the ledge, her heart beating wildly with hope. There was no one there.

Michel had heard her. "Aren't you sleeping, Justine?" he whispered.

"I could if only Star Boy would come back."

"You really like him, this young Indian friend?"

"Like him? I love him! He has been one of us for weeks! To me he's like you and Denis. My brother!"

Michel's voice sounded troubled. "Sometimes we have to say goodbye to those we love the most."

She thought he was speaking of their beloved family. "Michel, why did the fire have to come? Why did Maman and Papa and the babies have to go to heaven?"

He drew her into the circle of his arm. "We can't know everything, little sister. We must leave something to the love and wisdom of God. Sleep now. And we may find your Star Boy in the morning."

Curled up in the cradle of his arm, she felt safe, and she slept.

CHAPTER THIRTEEN

Farewell to Friend and Forest

"But where can he be? We've searched everywhere!" Justine sat on a rock the following morning, looking to Michel for direction.

"Indians know the ways of the wilderness better than we do," Michel assured them. "I know. I lived with the Hurons."

"You lived with them?" Denis kept close to his brother for safety. "Weren't you frightened?"

"Not then. The Hurons were my friends. When I was lost in the wilderness after I was left alone, they found me and took me in as a brother."

"Like we did Star Boy," Justine said.

"Like that, yes. And I think for now we'll call off the search for him and wait to see if he comes back to us on his own." Michel glanced quickly about the glade of spruce trees. "He may have his eye on us right now."

"I wish I could shout! I wish I could tell him to come back, that you've come to look after us!" Justine said without hope.

"Did he learn any of our language while he was with you?"

"Only a few words, and I don't think he knew what they were. It was a kind of game to him when we tried to teach him things on birchbark and on the ground."

"He talked away all the time in Montagnais and I couldn't understand a word," Denis said. "But he always pointed and made pictures, and that helped."

"And he was Montagnais?" Michel stood looking down at them. "You're sure of this?"

"What else could he be?" Justine wondered. "The Iroquois burned the village and left him there."

"Then we'd best leave him here, wherever he is, and go back to the cave for a while. He may yet come before the day is gone." Michel put his arms around them and urged them down the path.

"Will you tell us more of your adventures then?" Denis asked.

"Food first, adventures after," Michel promised. "We'll gather more plants and berries and use some of your meat to make a stew. You have a big *coureur* appetite here now, you know! We'll have to find more meat if this Star Boy of yours doesn't come back soon."

There was still plenty to eat but Justine was not hungry. She felt she could never be hungry again until she knew what had happened to Star Boy.

Michel looked at her with a worried frown. "If I tell you more of my story, will you try to eat later, at supper?"

"I'll eat when I know where Star Boy is. But please tell us where you went when you were left alone, Michel."

"With the Hurons, as I told you—living as an Indian, learning Indian ways, taking part in their rituals and ceremonies. And then one morning, after journeying with them for some months, we came to an astonishing place, leagues and leagues away from here."

"Was it the place with the spices and gold?" Denis asked eagerly.

Michel smiled. "Hardly that. The treasures in that place couldn't be measured in golden terms."

"What then? What was it?" Justine crept closer.

"It was a fort in the wilderness in Huron country. It was called Fort Sainte-Marie. You know how it was the Jesuit brethren who began the mission in our Tadoussac? This was their mission, too."

"Was it a fort like ours?" Denis asked.

"Smaller, but self-contained. A little village inside a log palisade with stone bastions. There were stables, barns, a cookhouse, kitchen gardens. There were workshops, even a hospital and a chapel."

"But they would be French there, just like us!" Justine realized suddenly. "They would take you in like one of them!"

"They did. I was taken on as one of the 'given', a lay brother to serve in the fort. Can you guess where I worked?"

Suddenly she recalled Old Granny Beauchamp and Michel's ways with healing. "In the hospital!"

"I did. While others looked after the cattle and pigs and poultry brought by canoe from Quebec, and did work about the log buildings, I tended the sick. And many of them were Indians. They were my friends."

"Were there Indian villages all around there?" Denis asked.

"Oh yes, and the Indians would come to the fort, down the footpaths through the forest, to be baptized and blessed and to be healed." He gave a deep sigh.

"Didn't you want to stay there?" Denis eyed him curiously. "I would. Some day I'd like to go and work in a place like that."

"Not in that place," Michel said slowly. "It's no longer there."

They waited, staring at him, not daring to question him.

"The Iroquois came." His voice was so low they could scarcely hear him. "They set the nearby villages ablaze and we knew our turn was next, so we fired our own fort and left." He paused.

Justine whispered, "What happened to all the people in the fort?"

"Some of them got away. Some of them were killed— among them the priests."

Denis gaped at him. "How could they do that to the holy fathers?"

Michel took his hand and held it tightly in his own. "Because they saw us as the enemy, because they saw their way of life in danger, a way of life they'd had for hundreds of years. And they saw the settlers and traders taking over their territory."

Justine said suddenly, "Do you remember Guillaume?"

"Papa's poet-philosopher from France? Yes, I do." His mood lightened. "He smacked the table so hard he made the dishes rattle!"

Justine laughed. "That's what I remember, too. But it's the way you spoke just now. You remind me of him. He blamed us and the English for bringing war to the tribes."

"We've brought more than war. You know the dreaded pox?"

How could she not know it, when it had swept through the settlement two years before and taken six lives— among them Old Granny Beauchamp, who thought she had a remedy for everything.

"Yes," she said, "I know the pox."

"And do you know where it came from?" Michel asked.

She shook her head, wordlessly.

"From France, on the sailing ships. Hundreds of Indians have died of that and other diseases we've brought. That's why I was happy to make amends."

"Make amends? What do you mean?" She looked at him, puzzled.

"By helping the Indians who came to Fort Sainte-Marie when their own medicines didn't bring a cure. Sometimes ours from France were the answer."

"But they know so much about plants that help sickness, Michel. Denis and I wouldn't be here now if it hadn't been for Star Boy."

Michel nodded wisely. "There's many a *coureur de bois* and priest and settler who wouldn't have survived if it hadn't been for the Indians. They taught us how to travel by snowshoe and canoe, they showed us how to grow Indian corn and to eat the food of forest plants and harvest the animals for food and shelter and clothing. They're the *coureur*'s friends in the wilderness."

"The next time you go to be a *coureur*, I'll go with you," Denis promised boldly. "I'll be grown up soon!"

"Not soon enough for what I plan, Denis." He watched their faces carefully for the effect of his words. "I want to go back to France and learn more about healing. Then I'll come back to New France and work as a physician in the settlements. I want to tell them in the old country how the Indians heal. Their ways are like Old Granny Beauchamp's."

Shocked, Justine stared at him. "You want to go back to France? What will become of us then, Denis and me? We'll have to go back to France too! And what will happen to us there?"

"Oh, no, Justine. There's someone waiting for you down there in our own village."

"Someone?"

"Your friend Gervaise, and all his family. He's been beside himself with worry over you, feeling it was all his doing."

Justine smiled a quick, secret smile. "I like Gervaise," she said. "He's always been my friend."

Michel tweaked her short boy's hair and grinned. "I think someday he hopes to be more. But for now his parents want to take you in and care for you as their own, you and Denis too."

Another thought occurred to her. "But what about Louis Gaudin? Shall I have to meet him in the village?"

"Never again, I hope. The ship with the widows and orphans arrived from France and he chose himself a bride from among them. They've gone to make a new life up the river at Trois Rivières. And that, I hope," said Michel grimly, "is the last we'll see of him."

Then she remembered the one whom, in the midst of Michel's story, she had almost forgotten. "But what of Star Boy?" She was almost shouting. "Gervaise and his family won't want an Indian boy! They have enough children already. I can't do this, Michel, I can't!"

Michel motioned her to silence. "He came while we were speaking. Be calm, Justine, or he'll fly again."

"Where is he?" She did not look but kept her eyes on Michel.

"At the end of the ledge, near the path. He came down as silently as a leaf in the forest. He's sitting on his heels, watching."

"Just as he did when he came back to us first," Justine whispered. "Then he had to learn to trust us before he'd live with us."

Michel willed her to look at him and would not let her gaze go. "I've had to trust a great deal, little sister, a very great deal. Trust those I thought to look on only as my enemy."

"What do you mean?" She stared at him, puzzled.

"I didn't tell you the end of my story."

"Were there more adventures?" Denis forgot Star Boy in his eagerness. "Tell us. Please tell us, Michel."

"I came down the Saguenay as a prisoner, not the way I expected to return home."

"A prisoner?" Justine was horrified. "How did that happen?"

"A small band of Iroquois captured me on the shore of the Saguenay, where another great river flows in."

She could not believe it. "But you're here!"

"They didn't kill you!" Denis said. "I thought the Iroquois killed everybody."

"Not always, Denis. I was a lucky one. It was a chief, Gosadaya, and a few of his chosen warriors. They had come on a private quest and left the rest of their band in encampment."

"But how were you safe?" Justine raised a hasty prayer. "Praise God you were!"

"I was able to bring them healing. The chief had fallen ill and was burning with fever. I had with me some of the medicines from France that we had used at the fort. Their own herbs had done no good; mine did."

Denis asked, "And he got better?"

"Completely. We had many with fevers to treat at Sainte-Marie, and among them were Iroquois, because we never turned any away who came to us, even if they wore the face of the enemy."

"That must have been where the smoke came from!" Justine remembered. "Did they come down this far?"

"Yes, they were on their own mission," Michel said solemnly.

"What was that? To attack our village?"

"No, not this time, not this chief and his band. Nor ever again, I think," Michel said.

"Why then? Why don't you tell us?" Justine said impatiently.

"I'll tell you, but will you want to hear?"

"Of course I want to hear!" She could have shaken him, brother or not.

"This chief and his warriors were part of the Iroquois band who came a month or so ago to attack the Montagnais here."

"The village where we found the food and all the things to help us," Justine said.

"The same, I think. But before they set off upriver again, the chief's son was stolen by the Montagnais, his young son of ten harvest moons."

"His son?"

"Yes." Michel kept his eyes on her own. "They came down to search for him. He'd lost two sons to the pox, and Little Eagle was the only one he had remaining."

She turned her face away.

"I think they are still encamped on the heights across the river, Justine."

Again she said nothing for a moment. Then she burst into a torrent of words. "But he's Montagnais! I know it! He's not Iroquois! He can't be! He lived with us as a brother and he's fed us and kept us safe! The Iroquois who tried to kill him came back to look for him!" She described what they had seen.

"It was a Montagnais who tried to kill him, no doubt of that. He came back on the sly to loot his own burned village. They do that sometimes." Michel rose slowly and faced the Indian boy on the ledge. He called out something in a tongue they did not understand. There was no response from the boy, only a look of puzzlement on his face. Then Michel called again, this time with different words and inflections. The boy sprang to his feet, an expression of astonishment and joy on his small face.

Justine still did not look at Michel or Star Boy. "He really is the chief's son, isn't he?"

"Yes. He didn't recognize the Algonkian language of the Montagnais but he understands Iroquois. He's overjoyed that I know his name."

Star Boy proved it by moving closer, eyeing Michel with wonder and worship.

Justine was not ready to give in. "But we can't send him back! He belongs to us! He can come with us to the village and I'll find a way to keep him, all by myself. He's my brother. I can't let him go!"

Michel pulled her to him and held her close. "And did his father not let your own brother go?"

"But that was because of your healing potions. That was to give thanks!"

"And what if it had been Denis who'd been captured? Do you think he'd be happy away from his own people, away from us and the ways of our French settlement? Wouldn't you want him set free?"

She tore herself from his hold and went to stand at the lip of the ledge. "But that's different. We aren't keeping him prisoner. Denis belongs to us."

"And Star Boy, Little Eagle, belongs to the Iroquois."

Little Eagle! Suddenly Justine remembered the huge bird Star Boy had drawn on the cave floor. An eagle, of course!

Michel was still speaking, gravely, solemnly. "Don't you think that if we let him return to his own people we may have someone in that tribe who will speak for us, for all white settlers, after the way you've lived together here in the cave? A white skin will no longer mean an enemy for Little Eagle."

Justine turned slowly to face him. A gleam of hope flashed in her eyes. "But we have no way of getting in touch with his father."

"Yes we have. We who have lived in the wilderness have a way to speak to one another. Smoke!"

Denis had been hovering near the mouth of the cave, his eyes wide with alarm at the urgency of their words. Now he came up to them. "Why are you so angry with one another? Michel is here and we can go home again!"

Justine's lips trembled. "Star Boy is going home, too."

"With us?"

"No, not ever."

"Not ever?" Denis's eyes filled with sudden tears. "He's not coming with us?"

"Michel says his father is camped across the river. He's Iroquois."

"Iroquois! But he can't be!"

"He is. We're sure of that. Michel called him by name and spoke to him in his own language. He's going home to be with his own people."

"But he won't want to go!" Denis reached out a hand as if he could somehow prevent it. The tears brimmed over.

Michel drew him close and held him. "Shall we see what he wants to do?" With a few quick words he called the boy to him. Quickly he told his story, pointing across the great gulf to the other side of the river.

A look of amazement and joy lit the Indian boy's face. He answered in a spate of excited phrases, looking where Michel had indicated.

Justine watched him, filled with sadness. "He wants to go, doesn't he?"

Michel nodded. "Yes. Truly I think he does." He cupped Denis's face in his hand. "You can be brave, can't you, Denis?"

"Yes, I can be brave." He hid his face in Michel's jerkin. His words were muffled. "I've been brave, haven't I, Justine?"

"As brave as one of the king's soldiers," Justine said, thinking how far he had come from King Dagobert, and of her own need for courage.

Denis stared from one to the other. "What shall we do then?"

Michel knew. "Go up on the cliff and light a fire for our message. We'll soon know if they're still there."

Justine picked up the bundle she had made with her cloak and went up to watch the other three gather brush to make the fire. She could not join them; she was nursing her own grief at what was to come.

Soon the smoke was billowing from the ridge top, and Michel, using the old caribou hide from the village with deft hands, sent his message across the divide.

They watched, motionless, for an answer. None came.

Justine's voice was scarcely more than a whisper. "They've gone."

"Perhaps not," Michel said. "We'll try again."

She eyed him fiercely. "Do we have to?"

"Yes, we must." He built up the fire with brush and again his message billowed above the treetops.

This time they had only a moment to eye the opposite shore. A series of smoke puffs rose on the still clear air like vapour from the whales in the river. Justine even thought she could hear a kind of wild shout ring out across the water.

Michel smiled down at her. "They've understood. They'll send canoes to fetch him."

"Where shall we go with him, then?" Justine tried not to look at Star Boy.

"We'll take him to the path down the cliff and let him go on his own. Look! They're setting out already!"

Even as he spoke, two canoes put out from the cove on the other shore, and this time there was no doubt—the shouts of celebration echoed up the river canyon from the waters far below.

They hurried through the forest to the path down the cliff that Star Boy had taken on the day of the moose. They all stood suddenly silent in the sun-dappled shade of the trees that edged the precipice. Then, in a swift unexpected movement, Star Boy came to Justine and knelt before her. Carefully he removed the thong with the duck's beak and webbed feet from around his neck and placed it at her feet. He looked up at her with a kind of puzzled sadness.

She knew at once what she must do. In a movement just as swift, she drew the ruby red necklace from beneath her shirt and, looking down on him with her eyes filled with love, she placed it gently around his neck. The beads caught the morning light and gleamed like a dozen suns in the dusk of the glade.

Star Boy stared at his gift, unbelieving. Then, with a strange cry, he was gone down the cliff, his toes catching all the holds with assurance and speed. When he reached the bottom where the canoes were drawn up on the shore, they saw him look back the way he had come. At that moment Justine saw the flash of the necklet like a ring of fire on his small, slim body. Then the Iroquois were gone, shouting their chant of rejoicing as their paddles swung in rhythm across the glistening waters of the Saguenay. Justine and her brothers watched in silence as the rescuing party climbed the opposite cliff. At the summit there was again a gleam of ruby fire. Was Star Boy looking back to say goodbye? She would never know. In an instant they were gone from view, swallowed by the dense forest of spruce and pine.

"Goodbye, Star Boy," she whispered.

She felt Michel's arm tighten around her shoulders. "This is right for him, little sister. I know he must have longed for his own people just as you have longed for yours."

"Yes, I know that now."

Denis's face showed his concern. "He'll be happy, won't he?"

"I think he is already," Michel assured him.

Justine was still staring across the vast expanse of river water. "Do you think we'll ever see him again?"

"Perhaps. When there is peace among the tribes. He may come with his father to the trading post, or to the great fur-fairs in Trois Rivières or Montreal."

But she knew that could never be. There was too much enmity between Algonkian and Iroquois, between settler and Indian. Star Boy would grow to manhood and she would never know what had happened to him. But, helping one another, they had survived the wilderness together. He would be a part of her life for ever.

Slowly she bent to pick up the hide thong with the duck's beak and feet, and hung it gently about her neck.

"Time to go," Michel said. "The village is waiting for news of you. And you'll be just in time for a fine festival."

"A festival?" Denis was overjoyed, sadness for the moment forgotten. "Is another ship coming from France?"

"No, but the governor himself is travelling by barge down the river with a company of servants and soldiers, all in their coloured uniforms and velvet waistcoats, with tricorn hats embroidered in gold."

"Will their ladies come with them?" Justine looked down at her own ragged and torn boy's clothing, picturing the noblewomen with their hooped dresses, powdered hair, and lace bonnets.

"I think they will," Michel promised.

Denis looked up at him in awe. "The real governor of New France is coming to Tadoussac?"

"Governor D'Ailleboust himself. He's coming to inspect all the settlements in the colony before winter begins."

"Will there be little sweet cakes?" Denis asked hopefully.

"Little and big, I expect, and feasting and dancing. For Denis and Justine too, to welcome them back from the wilderness." He grasped their hands firmly in his own. "Come along, we're going home."

For a long moment Justine looked back at the trail to the cave. Then she turned away. "Yes," she said, "We're going home."